CHASING LETTERS
By
Sarah Collings

CHAPTER ONE

Molly soaked in the tub, the shadow of the flickering candle dancing across the walls of her small bathroom. The aroma of lavender from a bath bomb filled the room. She remembered someone telling her lavender helped relieve stress. Maybe it was that, or maybe it was the fourth glass of Pinot. She leaned towards the latter.

She twirled her glass, watching the wine funnel like a small tornado. Sighing deeply, she closed her eyes tight, thinking of the day she'd just had.

She had woken up late for work that morning. As much as Molly hated to admit it, this wasn't uncommon. It's just what happened when you were a single, twenty-five-year-old girl with a dead-end job who lived alone.

Immediately realizing her mistake, she sprung out of bed and raced to the kitchen to look at the time on the stove. It was seven in the morning, the exact time she was supposed to be *at* work to help open the doors of the small diner she served.

"Shit!"

She ran around her tiny apartment, throwing things sporadically around her already messy bedroom as she searched for her work uniform. She sent her co-worker, Jacey, a quick text as she struggled to get one of her legs into her pants.

Be there in 20. Grab my section for me?

Jesus, Moll. Again? I just covered your prep work for you.

Please?

K. But you're tipping me out.

Ty!

She got her things together, fed her cat, Jax, grabbed her keys, jumped in her car, and headed off to work. Her tires peeled as she pulled into the parking lot of King's Diner.

King's was an old, rundown place made of red and brown bricks, with a wooden sign that read "King's" perched on the top, peeling red and white paint. It wasn't much to look at, but it was the most popular place in her small, desolate town.

She had tried to sneak past the manager's office, hoping her boss, Sam, wouldn't notice she was late. Again.

"Moll!"

Damn it.

Sam ushered her into the office. She tried to defend herself, but he didn't give her the chance. He went into a long spiel about responsibility, priorities, taking accountability, setting an example, and other things that she hadn't fully listened to.

Since she was a kid, she had a habit of unintentionally tuning-out when people talked about things that bored her. Despite this, she was incredibly talented at *appearing* as if she was listening—nodding, eye contact, blinking—when she hadn't heard a word. The only person who knew when Molly was fake or real listening was her dad. He would snap his fingers and go, "Hello? Lights are on, but no one is home!"

It wasn't until Sam handed her a write-up slip that she snapped back.

"What? Why?"

"Did you not hear anything I just said?"

Not wanting to admit she hadn't, Molly snatched the pen from Sam's hand. She scribbled a sad excuse of a signature on the paper and stormed out of the office.

Whatever. Can't get worse, right?

Wrong.

She was stiffed by four tables, her food wasn't coming out on time, and she got into a heated argument with one of her favorite cooks because she forgot to put an order in. She spilled a tray of drinks, sending them crashing and shattering on the ground. She was about to have a complete breakdown in the walk-in when Sam told her she was cut.

She walked out the backdoor to the warm evening June air. That was when her phone pinged. She glanced down at the screen, and stopped, startled by the name she was staring at. Bennie, her sister, whom she hadn't spoken to in two years.

Hey Moll. I tried to call you. Dad has passed away suddenly. Please call me ASAP.

Molly opened her eyes again in the bathtub, still clutching the wine glass stem. She took another sip, the last few moments of the night flashing through her mind like movie clips.

The phone call with Bennie. The first time she had heard her sister's voice in two years. Bennie crying. Molly seemingly unable to cry at all. Numb. Sam and Jacey, concerned, gathered around her. Molly told them in the blunt, stoic tone she had managed to master over the last few years, "my dad is dead." The eerily silent drive home.

A sharp jab ran through Molly's chest, like her heart was made of paper and someone had crumpled it into a tiny ball. She rubbed her fingers below her collar bone.

She wasn't the average, grieving daughter. She was angry, she was confused, she was consumed with guilt. She hadn't spoken to her dad in two years, either. Yet, in the same breath, she was relieved.

Molly, who had never been one to deal with emotions well, suddenly had to deal with *all* of them at once.

She stumbled out of the bathtub, her head filled with the sweet static feeling that only Pinot could give. She wrapped herself in a towel and grabbed her phone, closing one eye to help with her blurred vision. She had three missed calls and two texts from Jacey. *God, Jacey is such a good friend.* Molly didn't think she deserved her. She had a text from Sam and two from Bennie. She didn't have the energy to respond to anyone.

She put the phone down and glanced up at herself in the mirror. Her long, strawberry-blonde curls, wet from the bath, fell over her shoulders. Her green, almond-shaped eyes were gifted to her by her dad—or so she was told. Being the younger of the two sisters, she didn't have much memory of her mom, who left when she was two. Only on occasion had she seen an old picture of her. From what she could tell, Bennie looked just like her.

She studied herself fiercely, finding any physical trait of her dad's. She lightly traced her lips, her bottom protruding just a bit more than her top, her narrow nose, and her soft jawline. As she finished staring into her reflection, she watched a single tear involuntarily fall from her right eye for the first time.

CHAPTER TWO

Despite how it may have seemed, Molly didn't have a terrible childhood. Yes, she had a non-existent mother, but she never *felt* like anything was missing. Her dad was there for school dances, sports games, birthday parties, relationships, and graduation. She couldn't recall a time when she'd felt like she was "missing" something.

Her sister Bennie, however, had a bit of a harder time. Even though she was only three years older than Molly, she remembered a lot more about their mom, who left five-year-old Bennie with many questions. Questions that their dad didn't know how to answer, and, quite truthfully, never really did. As Bennie grew, she finally stopped asking.

Although Molly and Bennie were sisters, they had opposite personalities. Bennie was shy, submissive, and reserved. She followed all the rules, never argued with adults, and was petrified of getting into trouble.

Molly had a rebellious spirit. She was lively, fun, social, and the life of the party. She was also a spitfire with a knack for finding trouble and hard-headed—she wanted it her way or no way.

Molly's rebellious spirit cost her a relationship with her family.

***

"I *love* him!"

"Oh, for the love of Christ, Molly. You don't even know him!"

Molly and her dad, Michael, were in the living room as Molly broke the news that she was moving.

She had met Liam, on a dating app. After driving three hours north every weekend for three months to see him, Liam asked her to move in with him. Molly, before discussing it with anyone else, happily agreed.

Her dad sat on the couch while she stood in front of the television, blocking his view of whatever show he was trying to watch, assuring she had his attention.

"Yes, I do!"

"You fucking don't!" Michael threw his fists on the coffee table so hard the floor vibrated.

The room went silent. Molly had noticed Michael being rather snippy lately—losing his patience, getting frustrated with himself, her, and even Bennie. This wasn't his usual calm, relaxed personality. Molly figured he was having a mid-life crisis or something.

For him to scream the way he had at her was so paralyzing that even Molly, who always had something to say, stood stunned.

She stood her ground, but the heat of his glare pierced through her, her confidence diminishing. She looked him over and noticed his age. Thick wiry grays were peeking through his red hair and beard, and the corners of his eyes were met with crows-feet.

Michael exhaled deeply, his face and voice softening and rubbed his forehead.

"Moll, I love you. And I think you have so much more of the world to see. To move hours away for a guy you've only been seeing for two months is just—"

"Three months." Molly crossed her arms. "And it's what?"

"Asinine. It's stupid."

That was all Molly needed to finally snap. She spewed venom all over the room, screaming every and any terrible, hurtful word that one could say to a parent. Michael yelled, but to Molly, his voice was muffled. All she could see was red; all she could hear was rage ringing in her ears. This was the ugly side of Molly, and she knew it, but she had no control.

The worst mistake she made was when she uttered her final words to him. Her nostrils flared, and her chest heaved. She spoke quietly but menacingly.

"I hate you."

Those were the last words she could get out before her dad leaped over the coffee table, grabbed her by her shoulders, and ran with her. He threw her up against the living room wall, not hard enough to put her through it, but hard enough to make the family pictures fall off the wall and shatter onto the hardwood floor.

He put his face right up against hers, their noses almost touching. He had never in her life put his hands on her. He held Molly against the wall, her feet dangling above the floor. His breath was short and choppy, and his pupils were so large that his eyes almost looked black. Molly struggled to recognize him. It was as if something had possessed him.

"If I'm so horrible and you hate me, leave. Don't expect shit from me. Don't ask me for anything. Don't call me for anything. Go ahead and see how long you last," he said through clenched teeth.

After a few seconds, she watched the expression on Michael's face shift from anger to shock. He let go of her shoulders, walked back to the couch, and put his face in his hands. She stared at him momentarily before storming out of the living room. As she turned the corner, she nearly ran into Bennie, who looked like a puppy that had been caught chewing a shoe. She had been eavesdropping.

"Move," Molly said, shoving past Bennie.

"I know he shouldn't have done that. But—"

Molly turned and glared at Bennie. "Why don't you ever just mind your own business?"

Bennie put her hands up and took a step back. It was no surprise she thought her dad was right. She was the golden child; the straight-A student; the one in college; the sweetheart. Bennie could simply do no wrong.

That night, Molly packed trash bags with clothes and small necessities. She took one last look at her bedroom. Tears filled her eyes, but they refused to fall. She walked out of the house for the last time without an ounce of resistance or a goodbye.

If she had only known what would happen after that night. If she had only known that she and Liam would only spend a year and a half together. If she had only known that everything would come tumbling down when she made a stupid, drunken decision. If she had only known that after that she would lose every friend she'd made—except for Jacey.

If she had only known that her dad would be dead six months after her world crashed. Maybe she would have talked to him. Maybe she would have swallowed her pride and called. Most importantly, she might have chosen her last words a little wiser.

"I hate you."

CHAPTER THREE

Sam told Molly to stay home from work the day after her dad died—she hadn't planned on going anyway. She woke up on the couch at around eleven a.m., still wrapped in her towel. Her coffee table was littered with three empty wine bottles, leftover pizza she hazily remembered ordering, and a half-smoked put-out cigarette.

She felt something soft rub against her right leg hanging off the sofa, followed by a soft purr. Jax gently reminded her that he had been ready for breakfast two hours ago.

"Okay, buddy. Okay."

Molly sat up, immediately smacked with the rush of a hangover headache. She laid back down, rubbing her temples.

"Jesus."

She lay there for a few minutes before mustering the strength to get up again. She threw her legs over the side of the couch and sat up. She regained as much composure as she could and stood, eventually going to her bedroom. She threw on an oversized t-shirt and grabbed the bottle of Advil. She poured a few into her hand, popped them in her mouth, and took a swig from a questionable glass of water on her dresser.

She then went to the kitchen, where Jax waited semi-patiently for his breakfast. He weaved in-between her legs, mewing, as she scooped some food into his bowl. She had adopted Jax a few months ago from a shelter after she and Liam had broken up so she wouldn't feel so alone. He had undoubtedly filled a huge void, bringing out her softer side. He was a cute little cat, mostly black, with a splash of white on his front, left paw and big yellow eyes.

As she admired his cuteness while he ate his late breakfast, she heard a knock on her door. She ignored it, not having the energy for anyone. A few minutes passed, and there was another knock. Molly sighed. She opened the door slightly to find Jacey, a card in one hand and a bouquet of flowers in the other, half-heartedly smiling.

"Hey, Moll," she said, giving a sympathetic look. "I just wanted to stop by and check-in. You weren't answering my texts, so I got nervous. And you," she looked Molly up and down. "Look horrible. No offense."

Jacey pushed the door open, moved past Molly, and looked around. Molly could see Jacey trying to hide her judgment, but her face said it all. The apartment was a disaster. Molly walked over to the couch, sat down, and patted the couch for Jacey to sit.

"No work today?" Molly asked.

"Not until later. I'm working dinner," Jacey answered, now eyeing the coffee table.

Jacey turned to Molly and handed her the card and flowers.

"Here, these are for you. I thought maybe they would help."

Molly took the flowers and card and put them on the coffee table. She picked up one of the empty wine bottles, took it to the kitchen sink, and filled it with water. She returned to the living room and put the flowers into the wine bottle.

"What's the card for?" she asked, picking it up from the coffee table.

"It's for you. You know, since your dad passed away."

"So, it's a dead dad card? They make those?" Molly giggled, chuckled, and went into a full-blown laughing fit—hunched over, clutching her stomach, tears streaming.

"It's not a 'dead dad card,' it's a fucking sympathy card. And for the love of God, don't you own a vase?" She pointed at the wine bottle Molly had just filled with flowers.

Molly wiped the tears of laughter from her eyes. "I prefer dead dad card. And no, I do not."

Jacey was silent, and Molly peeked over at her. She had accidentally embarrassed Jacey, and now she felt sorry for her. She leaned in and gave Jacey a hug.

"Thank you. That was very kind of you."

Jacey's face softened. She was a pretty girl—long, pin-straight black hair, icy blue eyes and a perfectly formed jaw line. She was a bit of a ditz, but she meant well and had a heart of gold.

"So, now what?" Jacey asked.

Molly grabbed a piece of the left-over pizza and took a bite.

"Now what, what?" she asked, her mouth half full.

"I don't know. How are you feeling? Have you talked to Bennie? Are you going to the funeral?"

That was another thing about Jacey. She sometimes cared *too* much.

Aside from Liam, Jacey was the only one who knew the whole story about what transpired between Molly, her dad and her sister. Sometimes it was a blessing. Sometimes it was a curse.

"I feel okay, I think." Molly shrugged, trying to be vague, hoping Jacey wouldn't pry.

"You sure?" Jacey raised an eyebrow.

"Yeah, I'm sure. I don't really know how to feel. The last time I saw him doesn't exactly make me feel great."

She really wasn't sure how to feel. A part of her felt guilty, like she should have done or said something sooner or maybe never moved at all. Another part felt like she was mourning someone who had been gone for a long time. She was still angry at her dad. It's not like he had tried to make amends with her, either.

"Have you told Liam?"

Molly's body stiffened. His name still did that to her.

"Why would he care? He hates me."

Jacey brushed it off, catching the hint that Molly didn't want to delve into that topic any deeper. She put a tiny hand on Molly's shoulder, looking around the apartment again.

"I know, I know," Molly nodded. "It's a mess."

"Why don't you relax, and I'll help you get this place a little bit straightened up?"

Normally Molly would protest, but she knew she wouldn't win anyway, so she agreed. For about an hour, Jacey straightened up while Molly numbed her brain with funny videos on her phone. Finally, Jacey rejoined her position on the couch.

"Thank you, Jace. For everything. I appreciate it."

"That's what I'm here for."

Molly turned on the TV, and they sat quietly watching a Jersey Shore re-run when her phone went off.

Bennie.

Jacey and Molly had looked down at the phone simultaneously, but neither of them moved. After what felt like an eternity of silence and avoiding eye contact, Jacey finally spoke up.

"Are you going to answer her?"

Molly shrugged again, still looking at the phone on the table.

"I think you should."

Molly didn't know anything about Bennie anymore. She didn't know where she lived, if she had a boyfriend or a fiancé, or if her hair was still brown. As far as she was concerned, Bennie was a stranger.

The phone pinged again with a reminder of Bennie's text. *Damned iPhones.*

She picked up the phone and opened Bennie's text.

Hey. Call me when you have a sec pls.

Jacey stared at Molly, clearly waiting to hear what the text said. Molly locked the phone and put it back down on the coffee table. To her surprise, Jacey said nothing.

They watched a little bit more TV before Jacey decided to head out. She hugged Molly goodbye and told her to call if she needed anything. Molly locked the door behind Jacey, returned to the couch and sat down. She opened her phone and reopened Bennie's text. After staring at it for a few minutes, she hit the call button.

As if Bennie had been waiting for her call, she picked up on the first ring.

"Hey, Moll." She sounded sad. Tired.

"What's up?"

"How are you?"

"I'm fine. What's up?"

"I wanted to talk to you about funeral arrangements for Dad. Are you coming?"

"I don't know."

"What?"

"I said I don't know."

Bennie didn't say anything for a second. Molly knew she was being stubborn, but she couldn't help it.

"Why don't you come home, and we can talk? Maybe grab coffee or something?"

"I am home."

"You know what I mean, Molly."

Molly could hear the irritation growing in Bennie's voice. It made her feel partly giddy and partly stupid.

"Okay. When?"

"Do you work tomorrow?"

"My boss told me I could take off for however long I need, so I'm sure he wouldn't care."

"Why don't you meet me at LuLu's at 3:00? We can get lunch. I miss you."

LuLu's was a small, high-end café back in her hometown. It was the opposite of King's, and Molly winced at the thought of going there.

"Okay. I'll see you then." Molly hung up without saying goodbye.

Molly spent the remainder of the day trying to numb herself with shitty television and shitty food. Still, the thought of returning to her hometown kept creeping back into her mind and dropping forcefully to the pit of her stomach. She didn't want to go, but why? Was it shame? Guilt? Embarrassment?

Or was she just nervous?

Jax jumped onto the couch and rubbed his little head against Molly's chin. Molly smiled softly and scratched his head with her pointer finger.

"Oh no! Who's going to take care of you, bud?"

Jax chirped and purred, rubbing against her face some more.

Molly smirked.

"I guess I just won't be able to go meet Bennie. What kind of cat mom would I be to leave my baby to fend for himself? A shame, but priorities, ya' know?" She gave Jax another scratch.

Thank God she got this cat.

CHAPTER FOUR

Molly showed up that morning for work on time. When she walked in, Sam met her at the back door.

"Hey, Moll. I saw you pull in on the camera. I wasn't really expecting you today. You sure you're okay to work?"

"Yeah, I'm fine. It's a good distraction for me anyway." Molly half smiled.

"Okay. Well, let me know if you change your mind. It won't be a problem."

"Thanks, Sam," Molly said as she tied her apron around her waist. She joined Jacey to help with prep and cut lemons.

"Why are you here?" Jacey asked.

"I needed a distraction."

"So, what's your plan?"

"What do you mean?" Molly knew what she meant.

Jacey stopped cutting the lemons and swung her head to look at Molly, her long black ponytail gracefully flipping over her shoulder.

"C'mon. Why are you being so impossible? Are you going to see Bennie?"

"Oh. Well, I was supposed to go today. But I have a ton of responsibilities I have to worry about here."

Jacey scoffed. "Do you think this is the first time I've ever met you?"

Molly stopped cutting and looked up at Jacey, offended.

"What does that mean?"

Jacey motioned her arms up in the air and waved them wildly. "You work at this shithole diner as a server. This is the first time you've been *on time* for a breakfast shift in probably three months, I just cleaned

your entire apartment yesterday, and your *dad* just died.

What the hell do you possibly have to worry about that

is more important than that?"

Molly turned back to the lemons. "Jax."

"I'll take care of the cat, Molly. Go see your

sister. I can't believe I'm even arguing with you about

this right now!" Jacey pushed her hair away from her

forehead in frustration.

"Why are you so worried about what I'm doing,

Jacey?" Molly threw the knife down on the counter and

glared at her. She knew Jacey only had good intentions,

but she could be especially annoying with her constant

badgering.

"Because both of us know that you *know* what

the right thing to do is. You are just refusing to do it,

and no one else is going to tell you that you're acting

like a bitch!" Jacey picked up her cut lemons, threw them into the clear container and walked away.

"I don't need your fucking help!" Molly yelled back at Jacey, who didn't turn around, but did flip a middle finger up behind her, at Molly.

The diner opened, and a few older men who were normal Friday morning regulars came in and sat at the little breakfast bar.

"Hey, Molly! It's great to see you!" one of them said.

"Mornin', George!" Molly fake-smiled, pouring his coffee.

"How ya' doin', sweetheart?" George said quietly.

Not much stayed quiet around the town. Still, she didn't want to let on.

"Never better, honey," Molly lied. "What are you having? The usual?"

George always ordered scrambled eggs with two sides of pork roll, a side of home fries and a black coffee.

"I'm going to change it up today." George rubbed his chin and peered through his glasses at the menu.

Molly pulled out her notepad and pen, waiting patiently.

"I'll have the eggs benedict today," he said, smiling at her and handing back the menu.

Molly froze. In the past two years, George had never ordered anything other than his usual, and the one day he decided to switch it up, he switched to her dad's favorite breakfast.

Molly, Bennie and Michael used to go to their local Red Run Diner every Sunday morning for years. It's probably what sparked Molly's love for diners. They had the same religious order, she and Bennie would get chocolate chip pancakes, and their dad would get the eggs benedict. They would use crayons to play games on the kid's menu, and their dad never said "no" when asked to play tic-tac-toe. He always let them win, too.

"Molly?"

She snapped back to George, who still held the menu out for her to take. She wrote "eggs benedict" on her notepad and took the menu from him.

"One eggs benedict, coming up." She forced a haphazard smile.

When George's food was ready, she grabbed the plate from the kitchen and looked down at it. Her stomach turned at the sight of eggs benedict. She took a deep breath and returned to George, placing the plate in front of him.

"Enjoy," she said quietly, carefully placing the plate before him to ensure it didn't slip out of her sweating palms.

Molly continued for a few hours serving tables and collecting her tips. On her way to cash out one of her tables, the diner's front door swung open, and she looked up to greet the guest. Before she could get a word out, she choked.

She wanted to run. She wanted to pass out. She wanted to throw up. Instead, she stood dumbfounded, jaw practically touching the floor.

"Hey, Moll," Liam said gently.

Molly racked her brain for anything she could say, but no words came out.

"I heard about your dad. I'm really, really sorry."

Still nothing. She was screaming on the inside but paralyzed on the outside.

"Moll?" Liam waved a hand in front of her face.

"Yeah. Thank you."

Oh my god, that was the best you had!?

"I just feel horrible. I feel like I'm such a big reason you guys didn't talk, and I—"

"It's okay. I'm okay. Thank you. I gotta go, though. Super busy."

She rushed back to the kitchen, ripped her spare house key off her keychain and ran up to Jacey.

"Here."

"What's that for?" Jacey asked, taking the key into her palm.

"Jax. One scoop of food two times a day. Litter box is in the bathroom. Table eighteen and table sixteen are cashed out and finishing up. Take the tips. I'm going to see Bennie. Thank you."

She grabbed the rest of her things and called into Sam's office.

"I have to go. I'm sorry!"

"No problem! Let me know if you need anything!" Sam called back.

Molly rushed out the back door, ran to her car, and sat down in the driver's seat with the door still open. Her head spun, and her stomach turned. She took deep breaths, trying to regulate her heart rate and ease the nausea.

She started her car and headed back to her apartment. *Who the fuck does Liam think he is, just coming into my work like nothing like we haven't spoken in six months? A simple "Sorry, your dad is dead" text would have sufficed.*

Shit. She'd blocked his number. Maybe he had tried to text her. Why was *she* mad at him? She was the one who ruined everything. And fucking George with the eggs benedict. Really? Out of all the breakfast options he could have changed to, he had to pick eggs benedict. Her mind continued to race until she got back to her apartment.

She grabbed a bag, throwing in clothes, her toothbrush, make-up, and essentials. She didn't know if she was going to the funeral. She didn't know if she would stay overnight but wanted to be prepared.

She gave Jax a pet on her way out and looked around her apartment again before leaving. She sighed. This feeling was way too familiar.

"Be a good boy, Jax," she said, before walking out the door.

She walked out to the parking lot and jumped into her car. As she drove, she realized she hadn't been back to her hometown in two years, but she still didn't need a GPS. She knew the way by heart.

As the woods and trees started slowly diminishing and the homes grew closer together, Molly felt nostalgic, but not in a good way. Even though she grew up in this town, she felt like an outsider—like she didn't belong.

She glanced down at the clock—two forty-two. She still had about five minutes before she needed to be at LuLu's, but she knew Bennie would be there early, as always.

Molly found a parking spot a few blocks down. She pulled in, parked, and got out of her car, putting a couple of quarters in the meter. She walked to LuLu's and stopped when she got to the front of the cafe. It was a cute, white building with a white sign that read "LuLu's" in pink cursive. No brick. No tattered shingles. No peeling sign paint.

Ugh.

The bell on the door chimed as if announcing her arrival, as she walked in. She looked around for Bennie. She saw her in the back corner booth, waiting with a coffee in front of her.

Bennie looked the same. She was never one to put a fun color in her hair, get a spontaneous tattoo or piercing, or do anything different. She didn't have a ring on her left hand. She still had shoulder-length, wavy, mousy brown hair, not a split end in sight. She wore minimal make-up but was naturally pretty, tall, and slender, not shapely like Molly. She had the same almond-shaped eyes as Molly and Michael, but they were a deep brown, not green.

Molly walked to the booth and sat down across from Bennie. Bennie looked up from her coffee and smiled.

"Moll," Bennie said breathily.

"Hey."

Bennie got up, went to Molly's side of the booth, and hugged her.

"I am so happy to see you!" Bennie choked up as she spoke.

After far too much hugging for Molly's liking, Bennie let go, put her hands on Molly's shoulders, smiled, and then sighed.

"I'm not gonna lie. I didn't think you were going to show up."

Molly pursed her lips together as Bennie went back to her side of the booth. A waitress came around to take Molly's order.

"Just water with lemon."

There was a painfully long silence before Bennie broke it.

"How are you hangin' in there, sweetie?"

Molly hated it when Bennie called her sweetie. Bennie was only a few years older than Molly, yet she always tried to act like she was her mother, which irritated Molly to her core.

"I'm fine."

Bennie looked at her sympathetically, her chin lowering slightly as if she was trying to pull something out of Molly.

"What about you? How are you?"

"I'm trying my best. I'm sad and still in shock. I was the one who found him," Bennie said, her voice cracking.

"I haven't stayed in the house since it happened. I just swing by to get the mail. Everyone has been so supportive, though. We have so many flowers, cards, food, you name it."

We. Like they were sent for Bennie and Molly. Like they were sent for her dead dad.

"I just, I had no idea this was coming. Nothing can prepare you for something like this, you know?" Bennie made eye contact with Molly. Her deep brown eyes somehow became lighter as she let the tears fall.

Molly didn't know what to say, so she broke eye contact with Bennie and stared at the table. The server came back with Molly's water.

"Oh, god, pull yourself together, Bennie!" Bennie said, looking up and fanning her face with her hands. She took a deep breath.

"How did Liam take it?" she sniffled.

Molly forgot that Bennie didn't know anything that had happened between her and Liam. And she surely wasn't going to tell her right now.

"He's okay. He was busy with work so he couldn't come. He sends his condolences, though." she lied.

Bennie nodded understandingly.

They talked for a bit. Well, mainly Bennie. Bennie had a boyfriend. His name was Tyler, he was twenty-eight, and he was an accountant. *Riveting.* They had been dating for almost a year. He lived ten minutes outside of town, and they met during a charity walk for the county animal shelter. He had a kid, though, a three-year-old daughter, and according to Bennie, the kid's mom was a real piece of work. That added a little bit of spice to the story.

"So, are you coming to the funeral?" Bennie asked.

"I don't know."

"Molly," Bennie paused. "I know that the last time you saw him wasn't—"

"Don't. Don't even bring it up."

"You have to talk about these things, sweetie!" Bennie reached for Molly's hand, but Molly snapped it back.

There was that *"sweetie"* again.

"Bennie let's clear some things up. First, stop calling me sweetie. I am not your daughter, so quit acting like my parent. I'm only a few years younger than you are. And second, I don't have to talk about anything." Molly's voice was rising.

"Please, lower your voice. All I was saying was, you have no reason to have this hard outer shell with me. I know you're hurting."

"You don't know shit! I haven't talked to you in two years!" Molly was yelling now, and people were starting to stare.

Bennie's face turned red. "You're making a scene; please stop," Bennie whispered, looking around the room.

Molly laughed mockingly and sucked her teeth with her tongue.

"You wanna' see a scene? Here you go."

"Molly, *please.*"

Molly threw her hands down on the table, climbed onto the booth seat, and stood up.

"Hello, everyone!" She clapped her hands, gaining the attention of the other customers.

If all eyes weren't on her before, they absolutely were now.

"My name is Molly, and my dad is dead! Dead, dead, dead. Like—" She stuck out her tongue and made the slicing motion with her finger across her throat.

"But some of you know that, right?! Mrs. Parker, I know you saw me walk in. Why didn't you say hi!? I used to babysit for you. How are the kids? Hopefully not still stuck in this town, yaknowwhatimean?"

Mrs. Parker stared at her, horrified.

"And Mr. Witkowski! Long time no see, buddy! Don't think I don't remember that DUI charge from ten years ago!"

Bennie covered her face with her hands in pure humiliation. It only motivated Molly more.

"I know you all saw me. And not one of you, *not even one* of you, came up to me and expressed your condolences. Or hugged me, or fucking said *hello*."

The entire place was dead silent other than Molly's screaming.

"Why is that? Because sweet little Bennie here said that our front porch has just been flooded with cards and gifts and fucking fruitcake or whatever the fuck you rich, snobby, pretentious fucks like to make when someone dies."

People started to get up and walk out of LuLu's, but that didn't stop Molly from continuing her tyrant.

"Oh! I can tell you! Because I'm not Bennie. I'm Molly. I'm the one who left and never came back. I'm the one who you saw skipping class, chasing boys, and not participating in any of your cookie-cutter bullshit. I'm the one who ran off to somewhere I actually enjoyed, right!?"

She looked around the restaurant crazily.

"Well, fuck all of you!"

With that, she flipped two middle fingers, made the mic drop motion with her right hand, and jumped off the booth. She grabbed a twenty out of her wallet, slammed it on the table, and walked out. Bennie chased after her.

CHAPTER FIVE

"Molly!"

Molly walked steadily, ignoring her sister.

"Molly, stop!"

She didn't. Instead, she reached into her purse to pull out a pack of cigarettes and a lighter. She took one out, held it to her lips, and lit it.

"Since when do you smoke cigarettes!?"

Molly finally stopped and spun around to face her sister, who was breathless. Bennie stopped, too, seemingly stunned.

"I'm leaving," Molly said.

"What!?"

"I'm leaving, Bennie."

"You haven't even bothered to ask what happened."

Molly took a drag of her cigarette and exhaled.

"Don't care."

"Of course, you don't!"

Bennie began to sob.

"You don't care about anyone but yourself! That's all you've ever cared about! You didn't even ask. You didn't even ask what happened, you didn't even blink when I told you I found him, because you don't care! You're selfish, and you're mean!" Bennie dramatically fell to her knees.

Molly rolled her eyes at the theatrics. She understood Bennie was upset, but the ground-throwing was a bit much. She walked over and picked Bennie up by her arm.

Bennie hugged Molly, burying her face in her shoulder. Molly patted Bennie's back awkwardly. People walked past them on the street and stared, and now Molly was embarrassed. Finally, Bennie managed to gather her tears to just sniffles.

"Well, are you going to tell me?" Molly asked.

As if she had been a volcano waiting to erupt, in between sobbing, Bennie spewed everything. Their dad had died the night before Bennie called Molly. For a few weeks before he died, he'd been sick. Vomiting, headache, dizziness. He would have waves of intense happiness, followed by waves of intense rage, like what Molly experienced the day she left. Bennie stayed patient and pleaded with him to let her take him to a doctor. He kept telling her he was fine, and there was nothing to worry about.

The night he died, he was particularly sick, vomiting profusely and slurring his words. Bennie begged him to let her take him to an emergency room, but he refused, saying it was just a nasty stomach bug. She ran to the pharmacy to grab him medicine, and when she returned home, she found him face down on the bathroom floor, unresponsive. She called 911, but it was too late. He was gone.

"I tried everything. They made me do chest compressions; they made me check his pulse. His skin was blue. It was horrible. It was so horrible." Bennie's voice shook.

Molly threw the remainder of the cigarette on the ground and put it out with her foot. Despite her hard outer shell, she wasn't completely heartless. She felt sorry for Bennie.

"So, what do we do now?" Molly asked.

That was the ironic part. She didn't want Bennie to treat her like a child, but she had no idea what to do when it came to stuff like this and relied on Bennie for the answers.

Bennie sniffled and wiped her face. "I have to sell the house. I can't live there after everything I went through; it's way too much. But I need to clear it out, and I was hoping you would help me with that and the funeral arrangements. I don't even know if dad has a will, but if he does, I have to find that, too."

There was a long silence.

"Please, Moll. I can't do this one alone." Bennie's eyes filled with grief.

Molly took a deep breath. "Okay. Fine. Go get your car."

Molly followed Bennie to the house, gripping the steering wheel as she drove. Her heart pounded the entire way, and she could feel the sweat beading on her forehead. She didn't want to go, but after hearing what Bennie had gone through and seeing how distraught she was, she felt obligated.

Nothing had changed about the house since Molly had left, at least not the outside. The house still had light gray siding, a dark roof, and white shutters.

The front porch was the same, with the same swing swaying gently back and forth.

It felt as if she was dreaming. She expected to walk in and see her dad in the kitchen, cooking something like he always was, but she knew that wouldn't be the case.

She took a deep breath before getting out of her car and followed Bennie to the garage. They never used the front door, but Molly couldn't remember the garage code.

Bennie entered the code, and the garage door lifted slowly. Dad's car was there, and that's when it hit Molly. She was back home, and her dad was gone. Her vision blurred with tears. Unfortunately, but unsurprisingly, Bennie turned to look at her at that exact same time. She threw her arms open and wrapped them around Molly's neck.

"I know, sweet— Moll. I know."

Molly would have usually pushed her sister off her and told her everything was fine, but she embraced the hug, her tears quietly falling onto Bennie's shirt. Bennie began crying, too. They held each other, both grieving.

"None of this feels real," Molly said, muffled in Bennie's shirt.

"It doesn't feel real to me either, but I'm so happy you're here." Bennie finally pulled away, wiped Molly's face, and tucked one of her curls behind her ear. "I really thought I was going to have to do this alone."

When they regained their composure, the girls entered the house. The doorway from the garage led into the kitchen, and Molly took everything in. They really hadn't changed anything. The wall color, the furniture, the layout—everything was the same.

Bennie stood next to Molly, grabbing her hand to squeeze it gently.

"I've barely been here. I've been staying at Tyler's house. I don't know if I'm even ready for this."

Molly wanted to yell at Bennie again. There was a big difference between not being here for a few days and not being here for two years. She didn't say anything, though. Instead, she turned and looked at Bennie.

"What are we going to do?" she asked.

"Well, I was thinking we start in dad's room. Keep some things we want and donate what we don't want. Throw some stuff away."

Molly's stomach panged with hunger. She had forgotten she hadn't eaten anything at LuLu's, so that twenty bucks was a nice tip.

"I'm starting in the fridge. I'm starving," Molly said, walking over and opening the refrigerator door.

The fridge was packed with every food tray imaginable—fruits, veggies, edible arrangements, charcuterie boards, casseroles. She looked to the right of the fridge, and on the counter was a pile of sympathy cards and enough flowers to fill a greenhouse. She didn't want to check to see if her name was on any of the cards, but she did think about Jacey, who had been the only one to bring her anything.

In times like this, she wished they had extended family, but her dad was an only child, and her grandparents had died before she was born. It would have been great if her dad would have dated someone. She didn't know why he never had. Growing up, they would ask, and he would shrug.

"I have you girls. The only ladies I need!"

Molly took a green bean casserole from the fridge, put some on a plate, and heated it up in the microwave. After she ate, the girls went upstairs into the master bedroom, her dad's room. It was big, with a nice walk-in closet, an attached bathroom, and a big, king-sized bed, still neatly made.

Molly shuddered. Something about seeing everything so normal but so different was eerie.

Pictures of Bennie and Molly when they were little hung on the navy-blue walls. One picture stood out to Molly. It was of her and Bennie when they were kids, at the beach. They had buried their dad up to his neck in sand. They sat by him with their arms around each other, all three laughing. Molly smiled at the memory and then felt incredible guilt.

How were her last words to that smiling man in the sand, "I hate you"? It echoed through her brain.

"Would you mind going through the bathroom?" Bennie asked. I really don't want to go in there.

Molly nodded and handled the bathroom while Bennie went through Michael's closet and the rest of the bedroom. "I hate you" echoed through Molly's brain. She remembered his face. The anger. Being thrown against the wall.

Her thoughts were interrupted by Bennie calling out for her. Molly walked out of the bathroom and saw Bennie sitting on their dad's bed, holding a watch. It was the silver and black watch that their dad had worn every day. She handed it to Molly.

"Would you want this?" she asked.

"No, thank you. You keep it."

Truthfully, Molly didn't really want anything. *Who wants to remember this?* All she wanted was to clear out the house and go home.

The girls split up and did what they could throughout the rest of the house. Bennie worked downstairs while Molly worked upstairs. She avoided her old room until it was the last room left.

The door was shut. The colorful foam stickers she'd stuck on as a child held strong. M-O-L-L-Y, each letter a different color. Her dad wasn't thrilled, but he applauded her artistic ability.

With one big breath, she opened the door. The room was still painted light pink. On the right side was "the wall." The wall everyone had signed with a sharpie. She went over to it and traced the letters of old friend's signatures with her fingertip.

Her bed was still there, pushed into the corner by the window. It looked tiny compared to her queen-sized bed back home. Like her dad's bed, it was neatly made, like it was just done. Her dresser was in the same spot, and her mirror still had the heart she'd drawn in red lipstick.

The fact that her dad hadn't gotten rid of any of her stuff made her feel guilty for getting rid of his. Her mind flashed back to the last day.

Her body against the wall. His hands on her shoulders. The pictures shattering.

Fuck it.

Molly paced around her room aimlessly for a minute, then sat down on the bed and looked out her window at the view of their white picket fence-enclosed backyard. *How stereotypical.* She stared out, remembering once upon a time when she and Bennie had liked each other, playing as kids in the backyard, especially on summer nights like tonight. They would make up dances, play tag, and run around laughing and screaming under the purple and pink skies. They would catch lightning bugs and try to keep them in jars. Their dad would be cooking dinner with the windows open, and the aroma would fill their noses, indicating that the night was ending.

Molly's daydream quickly vanished when she heard an ear-piercing shriek from downstairs. She jumped up, rushed out of her room, and down to the kitchen where Bennie was.

Bennie stood, her face white, holding a piece of paper. She balanced herself on the kitchen table with her hand.

"What?! What's wrong!?" Molly yelled.

Bennie said nothing, still clutching the piece of paper in her hands. She stumbled into one of the chairs and sat down.

"You can't just scream bloody murder and then not say anything, Bennie. What!?"

"It's a letter," Bennie said quietly, staring at it intensely.

"Okay? From who?"

Bennie paused before she answered.

"It's from Dad."

"What?" Molly went to snatch the paper from Bennie's hands, but Bennie moved it back.

"You need to find yours."

"I need to find my what?"

Bennie broke her stare from the paper and looked at Molly, her eyes starting to water again.

"You need to find your letter before you read mine."

"How do you know I even have a letter?"

"Because it says it in mine."

Molly and Bennie tore the entire house apart, searching for Molly's letter but found nothing. Molly was beginning to think that her dad had written Bennie's letter right before he and Molly fought and said to hell with it. After an hour of searching, they sat on Molly's bed, exhausted.

"I don't think I have a letter, Bennie."

"There's no way. It says it in mine."

"Well, can you at least tell me what yours said?"

Bennie reached into her back pocket and pulled out her letter. She laid back on the bed, preparing to read her letter out loud, when they both heard a rustling sound.

They locked eyes and immediately started ripping the pillows off the bed. Sure enough, there it was, in the same kind of envelope that Bennie's was in. Her name was written in her dad's handwriting.

"TO MOLLY. LOVE, DAD."

"No way," they said in unison.

Both girls looked at each other again and started laughing—deep belly laughs. Molly took the letter in her hands, held it to her chest, and fell back on the bed, laughing even harder. Bennie was wiping tears, unable to catch her breath. They couldn't get over the fact that after an hour of ripping the house apart, it had been under the pillow the entire time. Why did they not think to check there from the very start? Why did it feel wrong to be laughing?

Grief does weird things to people.

When they managed to pull it together, Molly sat up and looked at the letter. She looked over at Bennie, took a deep breath, and opened the envelope.

CHAPTER SIX

Hey Moll,

If you're reading this, it means I'm no longer here. It also means that you've come home. Whether that means you came home before I died or after, I'm happy you're back, and I'm going to write this like you came back before I went.

I wasn't totally honest with you girls. I was sick and I knew something was wrong. I'm sorry I never told you, but I didn't want to cause a huge concern.

I started getting headaches. They started off mild but progressively got worse. I passed it off as just migraines due to age. They sucked, but I didn't think anything of them. I continued traveling, working, and going about normal life.

Then came the mood swings. When I was happy, I was great! I was myself. But when I wasn't, I experienced absolute rage. I hated it, but it was like I had no control. Almost as if I was watching myself from the outside, begging myself to stop, but something else had taken over. That's exactly what happened the day that you left.

Molly's heart sank.

I was sick, Moll. I didn't know it yet. And I am so, so incredibly sorry.

I'm sorry.

But I don't want to talk too much about that day.

After the mood swings came the vomiting, nausea, and dizziness. And that's when I finally decided I needed to see a doctor. I was referred for CT scans and MRIs. And I finally got the diagnosis after a few weeks. I had glioblastoma. The most aggressive brain cancer. The chance of survival was low. Glioblastoma is incurable. So even if I'd done surgery, chemo, radiation, and all that, the likelihood of me surviving for long wasn't great.

So, I had a choice. Either torture myself with a ton of treatment until I died or go enjoy my life before it was over. I chose the latter.

I went through all my old pictures of when your mom and I traveled, and I picked five of my favorite places that you weren't able to see that I wish you could have. I couldn't take you to these places because it reminded me too much of your mom. But you deserve to know about them. They're secret treasures.

Right after my diagnosis, I knew it would only get worse, so before I got too sick, I wrote seven letters. And for a few weekends in a row, I sucked up my pride and visited each of these places one more time. There is a special person, or people, at each place that has the letter waiting. But you won't know until you get there. They were the only ones who knew I was sick. They are expecting you. Each place is within driving distance (but not too close, don't worry). The place could be a restaurant, a bar, a mountain, who knows! You won't until you get there.

Molly giggled.

This is letter #1. It will take you to where letter #2 is. Letter 2 will take you to Letter 3, and so on. Chase these letters, honey. Chase all of them.

Upstairs in the attic is a safe. The code is 9-3-1-9-9-8

She gulped. *My birthday.*

In the safe is cash for you and your sister. There's $10,000. Use that for gas, food, souvenirs, whatever you want.

Let me make myself clear: I do not want a funeral. Something about people crying over my dead body really skeeves me out, haha! Plus, I don't need you girls worrying about expenses. In fact, don't focus on the house, my stuff, or any of the depressing dying shit right now. The only thing I want you and Bennie to focus on is how to get to the next letter and trust that everything else will work out the way it's supposed to. Dad has your back, even from the other side!

And Moll, if this is your first time back home, I need you to know; I'm sorry I didn't call to explain myself or apologize. I couldn't without telling you that I was sick, and I know how happy you are out there. I didn't want to ruin that.

Just know that I love you very, very much. And I am so proud of you for following your heart. Never stop doing that.

Love always,

Dad.

P.S. You're going to a small city called Shirlington, Virginia. It's about three hours south, give or take. Your hint for the secret treasure: tacos.

Molly put the letter in her lap and finally made eye contact with Bennie. She was embarrassed for everything she'd done over the last few days.

"I'm going to need to go get some more clothes."

The girls laughed, hugged, and then cried again. They spent hours in Molly's old room, reminiscing about their dad. They went downstairs for more food, took it back up to Molly's room, and snacked—like they had when they were kids. They never once let go of their letters.

Another hour passed before they remembered what their dad said about the safe. They went out into the hallway and pulled the string to bring down the ladder for the attic. The door creaked open, and the ladder unfolded for the girls to crawl up.

The attic was dark, dusty, and filled with old toys the girls begged for as kids, boxes filled with Christmas and Halloween decorations, and some of Dad's old tools. Bennie reached up and pulled the metal string for the light. Sure enough, in the corner was a safe.

Molly bent down on one knee and turned the dial. *9-3-1-9-9-8.* Inside was a thick, manila envelope with the word "Girls" on it. Molly reached in and pulled it out. She opened it up, and there it was—ten thousand dollars.

"Holy shit," Molly whispered. To see it in her hands made everything real.

"Why don't I hold on to that?" Bennie said, putting her hand out.

Molly rolled her eyes but obliged. She didn't feel like arguing with Bennie and had no room to, given her antics at LuLu's earlier.

"So, when do we leave?" Molly asked.

Bennie looked at the time on her phone—

eleven.

"Let's get some sleep. I have to text Tyler and

tell him to meet me here tomorrow morning."

"For what?"

"Well, I'm sure he would love to see these

places!"

Molly tilted her head, eyes widening in disbelief.

"Your boyfriend isn't coming, Bennie."

"Why not?" Bennie crossed her arms.

"Oh my god, aren't you supposed to be the

reasonable one? This money isn't for him, and I didn't

see anything in my letter that said, 'make sure Tony gets

his letters, too.'"

"His name is Tyler."

"Whatever. He isn't coming."

"Fine. But he at least has to come here in the morning and kiss me goodbye. Aren't you gonna tell Liam?"

Molly sighed. She thought about Liam and what it was like to kiss him. His face closing in on hers, her hand touching his face. Just as their lips were about to meet, she watched his face start to slowly morph into—

"Molly?"

"What?" Molly shook the image from her head.

"Aren't you going to tell Liam?"

"He'll be fine."

She did have to text Jacey and Sam and let them know it would be an extended trip, probably a week or two. She wasn't going to let them know why, though. Knowing her dad, this letter thing made complete sense to her. Since they didn't know her dad, they would likely think it was insane to go on a trip planned by a dead man.

Jacey texted back first.

No worries, Moll! Me and Jax are doing great! She sent a picture of her sweet little Jax.

Almost immediately after, Molly got a text from Sam.

Take as much time as you need. I'll be here if you need anything.

Molly laid down in her old bed that night to sleep, but she had a hard time. She missed her dad. There was no denying that anymore, but a rush of shame would overwhelm her any time she thought about it. She hadn't missed him for the last two years. Now that he was gone for good, *now* she missed him? Why didn't she ever appreciate anything while she had it?

She thought about how she hadn't set foot in this house in two years and how quickly life could change. She never thought she would be back in this town, in this home, in this bed.

She was excited to start their trip, but she was nervous. What were the secret treasures her dad was talking about? What if they couldn't find the letters? What the the hell does "tacos" mean?

Her eyes began to fall heavy as her thoughts slowly dwindled. She fell asleep clutching her letter to her chest.

CHAPTER SEVEN

Molly woke up the following day to the smell of
breakfast. She inhaled deeply, taking in the aroma. It
had been a long time since she'd woken up to that kind
of smell.

She sat up and rubbed her eyes, forgetting
where she was for a second. It all came back to her—
eggs benedict, Liam, the outburst at LuLu's, Bennie
finding their dad, the letters. All the events of the day
before were a lot for Molly to digest.

Speaking of digest, she was starving.

She walked downstairs to find Bennie over the
stove in the kitchen, making breakfast. She looked over
at the kitchen table to see a guy with slicked-back
blonde hair wearing a business-casual suit. He smiled at
her.

"Good morning!" Bennie yelled over her shoulder as she cooked.

"Morning."

She looked at the clock on the stove, 8:00. Way earlier than she preferred on a day off. She reluctantly made her way over to the table.

"Tyler, this is my sister, Molly. Molly, this is Tyler," Bennie called over again, flipping the sizzling bacon on the pan.

Tyler was okay-looking, but Bennie could have undoubtedly done better. He wasn't very tall, had a broad nose, and his eyes were larger than normal and close together.

"Nice to meet you. Very sorry for your loss," Tyler said, putting his hand out.

"Thank you." Molly pathetically shook his hand and sat down at the table.

"So, Bennie says you have quite the adventure ahead of you. What an amazing thing your dad did for you guys."

Man, this guy really hit the ground running.

Molly wasn't sure what to say back, so she close-mouthed smiled. She wasn't sure what it was about Tyler, but she already wasn't a fan. Bennie started bringing food to the table.

Why is she cooking? We're the ones who just lost our dad. Shouldn't Prince Below-Average cook something?

Bennie put Tyler's plate in front of him first, then Molly's. Scrambled eggs, bacon, and toast. *Original.* Molly didn't care; she was starving.

They ate in deafening silence for what felt like forever.

"So, you don't live around here?" Tyler asked, chewing his food.

Molly drew her eyes up from her plate.

"No." She took a bite of scrambled eggs.

Tyler cleared his throat. "W-where do you live these days?"

Molly looked up again. She had no interest in talking to this guy at a normal hour, let alone at this time in the morning.

"Not here."

Bennie kicked Molly's shin under the table.

"Ow, Benn—"

"Tyler, I told Molly about Grace!" Bennie interrupted, changing the topic of conversation.

Who?

"Oh! My daughter! Ugh, she is just the best. Her mom and I aren't, um, on the best terms, so it makes it a little bit hard to see her. But ya' know, the joys of co-parenting, right?"

"Mhm," Molly replied unenthusiastically.

"You want to see a picture of her?" Tyler didn't wait for a response before pulling out his phone.

When he faced it towards Molly, there was a tiny, pigtailed blonde girl on the screen. She had chubby cheeks, a big smile, and big blue eyes. Molly couldn't help but wonder how Grace was so cute with genes like Tyler's.

Tyler turned the phone back to him.

"And she just *adores* her future stepmom, Bennie."

Bennie swooned. Molly choked and coughed on a piece of toast. She had never pinned her sister as someone who could or would even want to be a stepmom.

"She has really been so therapeutic for me," Bennie said, not seeming to pay attention to Molly's coughing fit. "Something about a child's innocence.

They have no care in the world, no idea how cruel it can be." Bennie started to cry.

"Oh, honey, don't cry!" Tyler said, getting up and wrapping his arms around Bennie. "Think of the positives. I really don't think you should sell this place. It would be great for us three. Me, you, and Gracie. A little family."

"I don't know," Bennie said, wiping her face. "It doesn't feel right without him here."

Molly managed to get the toast down by chugging orange juice. Still coughing, she excused herself from the table and went upstairs to prepare for the drive. *Is this guy really in it for my sister? Or for a free house?* She shook the thought; she didn't have time to create more questions for herself. She packed up the belongings she'd brought, threw her bag over her shoulder, and headed back downstairs. Bennie and Tyler were already outside in the driveway, exchanging goodbyes.

She threw her bag into the trunk of Bennie's car and waited for the two to finish their obnoxiously long goodbye. They acted like they weren't ever going to see each other again.

Molly's phone pinged. She had a text from a number she didn't have saved.

Hey. It's Liam. I got a new number. I just wanted to talk to you about the other day. Do you have a sec?

Molly's stomach flipped. She quickly locked the phone again, putting it in her back pocket.

"Can we go now?"

Tyler and Bennie both looked at her, Bennie furrowing her eyebrows.

"Sorry. It's just that time is getting away from us."

Tyler nodded and kissed Bennie one more time.

"Text me all the time, okay?" Bennie whined.

"Of course, babe. Be safe. And have fun!"

Tyler waved as he got back into his car.

The girls got into the car, and Bennie whipped her head towards Molly.

"What the hell was that, Molly?"

"What was what?"

"Why were you so rude to him?"

"I don't know, dude. Something is off with him."

Bennie rolled her eyes. "Why? Because he isn't six foot four with a felony?"

"No. Seriously. Something is weird about him. And now he's talking about keeping the house?"

"Whatever. Maybe next time, try to be a little nicer. Put Shirlington, Virginia, in your GPS."

Molly saluted. "Yes, Captain."

It was three hours and forty-five minutes away—without stopping for food or the bathroom. As Bennie pulled out of the driveway, Molly took one more look at her old house.

I really hope you know what you're doing, Dad.

As the girls made their way through town, they passed LuLu's. Molly winced. She really had made an ass out of herself. *Fuck Mr. Witowski.* He was her ninth-grade math teacher, and he was notorious for being a dick. He deserved that DUI-blow. She was surprised *he* hadn't skipped town.

They passed by the hair salon that Renee owned. Molly used to go there to put purple highlights in her hair, and Renee always loved it.

"It's just so different from what everyone else does! It makes my job fun!" she would tell Molly.

They passed the local Lukoil. It was known for having the cheapest gas and selling cigarettes to minors. That's where Molly would go when she was a teenager.

They passed Pizza Heaven, which had the best pizza in town.

"Does Giuseppe still own that place?"

"Mhm! He'll never sell it. His wife says they'll have to wheel him out of there one day in a hearse." Bennie chuckled and then abruptly stopped.

They passed ShopRite. Molly had forgotten that there were name-brand stores out there, and she laughed at its size compared to her home market.

Home. A sadness washed over her. She missed her shitty diner, her shitty apartment, her shitty market. She missed Jacey, Jax and Sam.

She shook the thought off when they got to the highway.

"We need music!" Molly said.

"Eh, I really need to focus on driving."

"Who can't drive and listen to music at the same time?"

"I don't know where I'm going, Molly!"

"Me either, Bennie!" Molly said, mocking Bennie's tone.

She grabbed the auxiliary cord and plugged her phone in. Scrolling through her music, she came across their dad's favorite song. *I've Been Everywhere* by Johnny Cash. She hit play.

Bennie looked over at Molly knowingly and smiled. She reached for the volume knob and turned it all the way up. The girls sang their hearts out.

"I've been to Reno, Chicago, Fargo, Minnesota…"

"I've been to Boston, Charleston, Dayton, Louisiana…"

"I've been to Pittsburg, Parkersburg, Gravelbourg, Colorado…"

"I've been everywhere, man. I've been everywhere."

For a brief minute, it felt like their dad was in the car singing with them. Molly looked out the passenger side window and saw a small plane making a heart in the sky.

I love you, too, Dad.

CHAPTER EIGHT

Somewhere at a rest stop, Molly sat at a table that desperately needed to be wiped down, sipping a watered-down iced coffee while Bennie used the bathroom.

It was quiet, with only Dunkin Donuts, a McDonald's, an Auntie Anne's, and a small gift shop. The walls and floor were gray, and the sun beamed through a skylight in the high ceiling above her.

She looked down at her phone and reread Liam's text message. She didn't know what to say back. She didn't want to talk about seeing him the other day. She really didn't even want to remember it.

There was nothing to justify what she'd done. In fact, he'd been the ideal boyfriend. He bought her roses without being asked, took her out on dates, surprised her with small gifts, and always held the door for her. He was kind, soft and romantic.

But that was the thing. Molly hadn't fallen in love with kind, soft and romantic. Before Molly and Liam moved in together, Liam was fun. She fell in love with his spontaneity, dark humor, passion for adventure, and trying new things. After a year and a half, things became mundane. There were no more spontaneous day trips, dates were always planned, so was sex. His sense of humor went from "dark" to "dad." She didn't even like roses that much. She was appreciative, but she was *bored*.

"You ready?"

Bennie had come out of the bathroom and was ready to get back on the road.

"Yeah. You want me to drive?"

Bennie laughed. "Absolutely not."

"Why not?" Molly pouted.

"Because I'd like to actually see these letters."

They had about an hour and a half until they reached Shirlington, Virginia. Then they'd have to figure out what "tacos" meant.

Molly reclined her seat and closed her eyes, drifting into a nap. While napping, she dreamt her dad was in the car with them. He was driving, and Molly and Bennie were in the back seat, like kids. He kept looking back at them and smiling but never spoke. Molly tried to touch him, but she couldn't feel anything. He winked at her.

She woke up from her dream to Bennie shrieking. Molly jumped, startled.

"We're here!" Bennie sang, clapping her hands.

Molly rubbed under her eyes and saw a white sign with green lettering.

"Welcome to Shirlington!"

She straightened up in her seat and stretched her arms above her head, looking out at the city. It was quaint, nothing like the cities she was used to. There were a ton of restaurants and cute stores, some people walking dogs on the brick sidewalks, others eating outside at tables with umbrellas shielding them from the summer sun, exchanging laughs and sharing appetizers.

They passed a sports bar called "Patty's." Molly nudged Bennie and nodded in the direction of the bar.

"Wanna get a drink?"

"It's barely one-thirty in the afternoon. Did you forget what we came here for?"

"Well, at least park the car so we can get out and walk around a little."

Bennie found a parking spot and pulled in. The girls got out of the car, stretching their legs. Molly looked up and saw big buildings towering over her. They weren't skyscrapers by any means, but they did make her feel small.

Bennie pulled Letter #1 out of her purse and scratched her head.

"Tacos...Tacos..."

"I'm just going to start walking," Molly said.

"Why don't we google tacos? Maybe that will give us a clue?"

Molly turned to her right to see a gentleman in a business suit walking past her.

"Excuse me?" Molly reached out and gently touched the man's shoulder.

The man removed a headphone from his ear.

"Yes?"

"My sister and I are *really* craving tacos right now, but we aren't from around here. Is there anywhere that you would recommend?"

"Oh, that's easy. T&T. It stands for tacos and tequila. Go up two blocks and make a left onto Campbell. You can't miss it."

"Thanks!"

The man walked away, and Molly looked back at her sister.

"I'm making a rule for this adventure. No googling."

"Molly, that's insane."

"Nope! No googling!" she yelled back as she took off in the direction the man had pointed her. She wasn't sure if this was the right place, but she was going to find out.

They followed the man's instructions until they came across T&T. People of all ages were sitting out front at tables enjoying the food. The door was propped open, and a chalkboard sign with bright neon colors was out front. One of the specials for the day was a mango margarita.

Oh, hell yeah.

As they approached the front door, Bennie froze.

"What's wrong?" Molly asked.

"What are we supposed to say?"

"Don't worry. Leave it to me."

CHAPTER NINE

T&T was right up Molly's alley. Some tables by the windows had basket swings for chairs hanging from the ceiling, and others had bright pink stools. The ceiling was decorated with colorful string lights and the walls with Spanish comics and old advertisements. The purple, black and pink walls made the place pop.

The girls walked up to the counter and were greeted by a young guy, probably around their age.

"Hi, welcome in! What can I get started for you?"

"Hey. My name is Molly, and this is my sister, Bennie. Our dad is dead and—"

"Molly!" Bennie interrupted.

"What!?"

"You can't just start it off like that to a stranger! We don't even know if this is the place," Bennie signed, rubbing her forehead with her palm.

"Sorry about that. I'm Bennie, and this is Molly. Our dad left us a letter and—"

"Oh, so that's better? Instead of just getting to the point, you're going to tell the stranger how our dead dad wrote us a letter and give him the whole run down for thirty minutes?"

"Are you Michael's daughters?"

Both girls turned and looked at him, wild-eyed.

"Y-yeah." Bennie stammered.

The guy laughed, followed by a look of sadness as if he had realized why they were there. He was tall and thin. He was Spanish, with short, dark hair and a huge smile. He had a tattoo of someone's name on his forearm.

"I'm Luis. Your dad was an incredible man. He helped my mom save this place from shutting down years ago."

"How?" Molly asked.

Luis looked at the time on his phone and the line of people building up behind the girls.

"I get done in an hour. How about I get you girls some food and something to drink, and when I'm done, I'll come sit and talk with you."

"Yes, please." Molly smiled.

The girls looked over the menu and placed their order with Luis. Molly got the shrimp nachos, and Bennie got the pork tacos.

"Oh, and a mango margarita, please," Molly requested.

"I'll have a pep—"

"*Two* mango margaritas, please." Molly said.

Luis nodded and walked back to the kitchen to get their order started.

Naturally, Molly had picked the table with the basket swings. After a little while, Luis brought beautifully displayed food and margaritas. The girls finished their meals, sipped their margaritas, leaned back in their swings, and chatted while they waited for Luis.

"I can't believe it was that easy," Bennie said, sipping her drink.

"What?"

"You asked a stranger on the street where a good taco place was, came here with no information, and met the person we were supposed to meet first shot. It just all seems a little coincidental, no?"

Molly shrugged. "I guess so. But who cares? We made it, didn't we?"

"Yeah, I guess so."

Finally, Luis came back with three mango margaritas on his tray. He walked over to the table, put the margaritas down and took off his apron, bundling it up and putting it into the back pocket of his jeans.

"It's bittersweet that you're here. I knew one day it was coming, just never when. I would hold my breath any time there was a new customer I never saw before. It does bring me a little comfort that your dad and my mom are together again."

Molly frowned, empathizing with Luis.

"I'm sorry," Bennie said softly, touching his shoulder.

"Oh, it's okay. It happened about two years ago. My mom left it to me to run this place, and if it wasn't for your dad, I wouldn't have even had the opportunity." He pointed to the tattoo on his arm. "Maria was my mom."

Molly envied Luis a little bit. While his mom dying was just as sad, he got closure. He got to say goodbye. Her dad hadn't left them that option. She shook her head, trying to ignore those thoughts, and took another sip of her drink.

"This place didn't always look like this! My mom was close to shutting it down for good."

"What happened?" Bennie asked.

"I was only a couple of months old. My dad left me and my mom with a ton of debt, sunk into the restaurant. It was their dream to open it, and my mom never gave up on that dream, but financially she was struggling and almost didn't have a choice."

Molly and Bennie continued listening, intrigued.

"My mom used to say your dad had a love for the broken and different. He came here alone while traveling and took a chance on the food. He was the only customer that day.

"He told her how delicious the food was and asked why there weren't any customers. My mom broke down and explained everything to him. Until the day she died, she always said she didn't know what possessed her to do that. She wasn't someone who just threw their problems at other people. She was prideful. But she was so happy she decided to confide in Michael that day."

Luis took a moment. Molly could see he was trying to regain some composure.

"Your dad said that he would make her a deal. He would come here every weekend and help build this place into her vision for a small payment of pork tacos." He smiled, looking at Bennie.

"My mom refused. She didn't want pity help. So, he thanked her, paid for his food, and left. The next weekend he came back with tools in hand. He said he couldn't let the world miss out on this food because of something as simple as the looks of it. Every weekend for a month, he came down here, rebuilding this place. And what you're looking at now... your dad created."

Molly took another look around the restaurant. She beamed.

"This is amazing," she said softly.

"It is. Once the building was remodeled, people started flying in like crazy. My mom had to hire more staff, get more supplies. As I got older, I started to work here, and when I finally got to meet your dad, I felt like I was meeting a movie star. And I'll be damned if my mom ever let him pay for pork tacos ever again."

The three of them laughed together.

Luis reached into his other pocket, pulled out an envelope and placed it on the table. Molly's chest tightened. On the front of the envelope, in her dad's writing, was "Letter #2."

"When he came in and told me he was sick, I felt like I was losing a parent all over again. But this letter idea he had… I wish my mom would have done that for me."

Molly lowered her eyes and bit her cheek. She shouldn't have felt jealous earlier. Even though Luis got closure with his mom, that didn't make his situation any more or less difficult. He was in the same boat as her and Bennie.

"I *was* given some rules, though."

The girls laughed. *Of course, he was.*

"First rule is you can't take off to the next place tonight."

Molly and Bennie nodded.

"Second rule is, I have to show you around Shirlington."

"Okay," Molly said, waiting for the next rule.

"Third rule is," he slid the envelope back closer to him. "You aren't allowed to open this until you're back in your hotel tonight."

The girls groaned.

Luis put his hands up innocently. "I don't make the rules; I'm just enforcing them!"

They enjoyed the rest of their margaritas and left T&T. The first place Luis took them was Shirlington Park. It had a walking path and gorgeous scenery. To the right was an open field with a children's playground, and to the left was a large stream with cedar water. They could hear the water flowing. Small kids with their dogs played and splashed in the water, their moms sitting on the side smiling, watching, and waving.

Molly stopped and turned towards the stream.

"What are you doing?" Bennie asked.

"It's hot."

The late afternoon sun beamed down on them, and she could see the beads of sweat dripping from Luis and Bennie's foreheads.

"Don't do it," Bennie said.

Like a little kid who'd just broken the rules,
Molly ran past the moms sitting on the side and jumped
into the stream, splashing, and giggling manically. A
border collie ran up to her, jumping and splashing
along.

"Jasper! Jasper, come!" one of the moms yelled.

"He's fine! Just enjoying the water!" Molly
yelled back, waving.

Luis looked back at Bennie, smirked, and
shrugged. He followed Molly's lead into the stream. The
two of them tried to keep their balance on the slippery
rocks, falling and laughing. Bennie stood on the side,
shaking her head.

"C'mon, Bennie! You won't regret it." Luis
called out.

"No thanks, I'm good!"

Bennie always had a hard time loosening up.
Molly remembered when they were kids, and their dad

took them to a local lake back home. Their dad had the genius idea of letting them rent a kayak and take it out while he hung back on the sand. Bennie, terrified of drowning and whatever was lurking in the lake, wore a life vest.

Molly insisted on paddling as far out in the lake as possible. So far that the beach became nothing but a distant blur.

"Molly, we shouldn't be out this far. Can we please go back?"

"What's wrong?" Molly asked, grinning. "Don't want to fall in?" She swayed her body, rocking the kayak back and forth.

Bennie gripped the edges. "Stop it. No, I don't want to fall in."

Molly swayed again, the kayak teetering even more. "Don't want the fish to get ya?" She laughed, poking Bennie's ribs under her life vest.

"Molly, knock it off. I'm serious!"

Molly stood up on the kayak and swayed so hard that water began to pour in. Bennie let out a blood-curdling scream before she, panic-stricken, threw *herself* off the kayak into the water. She spit, coughed, and gagged as Molly hit the kayak floor, curled into the fetal position, tears of laughter pouring down her face.

"Why don't you ever listen to me?! Why do you always take it too far!?" Bennie screamed, pounding the water with her fists.

Molly giggled at the memory and looked at Bennie, who must have recognized the mischievous glimmer in Molly's eyes.

"No. Do not. Do *not*!" Bennie took a step back.

Molly ran out of the stream chasing Bennie, who was screaming at the same pitch she had when she was the ten-year-old on the kayak.

Molly grabbed Bennie from behind, holding her arms in towards her chest and moving back in the direction of the stream. Bennie yelled and protested the entire way down, trying to dig her feet into the ground, but Molly was too strong. Soon, she found herself in the water, too.

"There. Are you happy? I'm in." Bennie crossed her arms.

"Not yet!" Molly bent down, cupped her hands, and splashed her sister.

Bennie threw her hands up to defend herself from the splash. "Why do you always take it too far!?"

Molly swallowed those words hard. The kayak memory wasn't as funny anymore. She was only having fun, but maybe she did take it too far.

Luis interrupted and splashed both of them. This seemed to snap Bennie out of her annoyance, and she giggled, splashing him back.

Oh, so it's okay when Luis does it.

There were three grown adults in the stream, laughing, screeching, splashing, chasing each other, slipping, falling, and carrying on without a care in the world, like children.

The hot sun dried them off quickly as they got out of the stream and continued to walk through the park. Big pink and white flowers grew on the trees, making the scenery more colorful and livelier. Luis greeted anyone who walked by them with a friendly smile and a "hello." Bennie and Molly started to catch on and began doing the same thing.

As they walked, the three talked more about their parents and their lives. The girls learned that Luis's mom, Maria, was from New York City. She had met his dad when they were teenagers, both aching to escape the busy city life but not wanting to live in a full-blown suburb. That's when they found Shirlington, a perfect mix of both.

When they were eighteen, they moved there against their parents' wishes. Luis's dad bought T&T to fix it up, but Maria became pregnant a year after moving to Shirlington. Six months after Luis's birth, his dad wanted to move back to New York, but his mom enjoyed living in Shirlington. His dad packed up and left him and his mom with nothing but the debt from the restaurant.

Molly shuttered at how eerily similar some of his story was to hers. An absent parent and now a dead one. She admired the pride that shone in Luis when he talked about Maria. She hoped that one day someone would shine when they talked about her.

After leaving the park, Luis took them to a little shop called Nan's Gift Shop. It was run by a sweet older woman with wiry gray hair, rosy cheeks, and glasses.

The store was filled with small handmade souvenirs, candies, and gifts. Molly bought some chocolate-covered pretzels, and Bennie bought a "Virginia is For Lovers" t-shirt.

Once they left Nan's, Luis asked if they wanted to check out another bar. Night had fallen on them, and the city was getting busier. Bennie enthusiastically agreed, which Molly found odd. Bennie wasn't a drinker or big into night life. She would have expected a protest.

"Really? You want to go out?"

Bennie glanced over at Luis and cleared her throat. "Yeah, I do. I'm not a prude."

"No one says prude anymore. But okay, wild child. Let's go."

Luis led them to a small bar on one of the corners. The sign that read "Patty's Dive" was lit red. It was the same place Molly had tried to get Bennie to go to when they first arrived.

The bar was packed with people. The place didn't look very big from the outside, but it was huge inside. It had two floors; six giant televisions and four small ones aired a football game. The room echoed with a sports announcer's voice blaring through the speakers.

"Touchdown!"

The bar crowd roared, high-fiving and hugging. Sports weren't really Molly's thing, and neither were sports bars. She didn't understand why people made such a big deal about it.

They managed to find a few seats at the bar and sat down. Luis must have been able to read Molly's face because he looked at her and laughed.

"They have some of the best drinks in town. Just give it a shot."

A bartender came around and gave them menus with many drink options. Luis ordered a fancy cocktail with pomegranate and tequila, and Molly ordered the same. Bennie struggled to make a choice.

When the bartender came around with Molly and Luis's drinks and Bennie still hadn't decided, Molly took matters into her own hands.

"She'll have a vodka cranberry."

"I don't know if I like that."

"You've never had a vodka cranberry?" Luis asked.

Bennie straightened up in her seat. "I usually just drink wine at home."

Molly rolled her eyes at Bennie's bald-faced lie but decided to shut up.

"It's the blandest drink on this menu. You'll like it, trust me."

As Molly had predicted, Bennie liked the vodka cranberry. She liked it so much that she had six. Six vodka cranberries for someone not used to drinking was more than enough. Six vodka cranberries for Bennie released a side of her that Molly had never seen.

After vodka cranberry number three, Bennie let loose, laughing, and carrying on. She got louder with each drink. She played music on the TouchTunes and sang at the top of her lungs, whipping her hair around. Luis and Molly joined in, laughing.

"So, where are you staying?" Luis asked Molly.

"Oh. I actually hadn't thought out that far. I got distracted. This is honestly the most fun I've had in a while."

She looked at her sister, who was still dancing wildly on the bar stool.

"And clearly, this one really needed to get out. Bennie, sit down!" Molly scolded.

"No!" Bennie yelled back like a toddler refusing naptime.

Luis looked back at Bennie, threw his head back and laughed. "Your dad would be happy to hear that. She's an interesting one, isn't she?"

"That's one way to put it. Bennie! Sit!"

Bennie grinned and flashed a middle finger at Molly. Molly put her fingertips to her forehead and smiled.

"Well, there's a pretty nice hotel a few blocks away from here. Do you want to look it up?" Luis suggested.

Thankfully, the hotel Luis recommended had rooms available. It looked nice enough for them to rest their heads for a night, so Molly booked a room.

The night continued smoothly. Bennie continued to act like a fun, average girl in her twenties, and Molly, while occasionally scolding Bennie, was enjoying it. Seeing Bennie relax and have fun was— different. Refreshing. Occasionally, she would watch

Bennie bat her eyelashes at Luis a bit too hard, and Luis would reciprocate in the flirting. Molly didn't intervene, though. She thought it was kind of cute.

At one point, Luis whispered something to Bennie. She blushed, playfully batted his shoulder, and whispered something back.

When Bennie asked for vodka cranberry number seven, things took an unexpected turn.

"I'm sorry, hon, but no more tonight." The male bartender shook his head.

"Why not?" Molly asked.

"She's clearly drunk. I can't, in good conscience or at the risk of sacrificing our name and liquor license, serve her anymore."

"Oh, please, she's *fine*. Look at her!"

Molly, Luis, and the bartender all turned and looked at Bennie, who was swaying in her chair, unable to focus her eyes. She slouched over the bar, holding her head up with her hand.

"Yeah!" Bennie slurred. "I am." She hiccupped and held up a pointer finger, waving it aimlessly. "I am compleeetely fi—"

She vomited all over the bar. Other customers quickly rose from their seats, screaming, yelling, and running.

"Oh, fuck!" Molly yelled.

"Oh, noooo! I didn't mean to do that. I'm not a prude, I sweeeaaar!" were the last words Bennie managed to slur before her head hit the bar.

Molly grabbed the envelope of cash out of Bennie's purse and threw some money on the bar. She grabbed the purse as Luis picked Bennie up and threw her over his shoulder, not seeming to care about getting vomit on him.

"Sorry about the mess! You're a great bartender! I tipped well!" Molly yelled across the bar.

The bartender glared angrily and yelled something, but it was too loud, and Molly was too far away to hear him.

Luis and Molly ran out of the bar, laughing the entire way.

"I am so sorry," Molly panted. They had gotten far enough away from Patty's to walk instead of run.

"It's honestly fine. I serve margaritas all day. This is nothing I'm not used to."

"I'm sorry, tooooooo!" Bennie sang out, her body flopped over Luis' shoulder, her head bouncing against his back as they walked.

Luis laughed and patted Bennie's back.

"No worries! I'll just never be allowed in Patty's ever again. You'll feel this tomorrow, though, and that might be worse!"

They reached the hotel and checked in, making their way up the elevator to the third floor. They got to the room, and Molly scanned the key. Two queen beds were neatly made, practically calling her name. Molly couldn't wait to lie down.

"Where should I put the precious cargo?" Luis asked.

"On the bathroom floor?"

They laughed. Luis put Bennie into one of the beds, and Molly put a trash can next to her, just in case.

"It was really great hanging out with you guys tonight. I'd expect nothing less from Michael's daughters. It's funny because I can see him in both of you but in different ways."

"We had a great tour guide. Thank you for everything, Luis."

The two exchanged a hug. For a moment, Molly forgot that they'd just met. She felt like they had been friends forever.

Luis grabbed the letter out of his pocket and handed it to Molly. She nodded over to Bennie.

"Wait til' the morning. She'll want to read this, too."

Molly took the letter and tucked it into the nightstand drawer between the two beds. She and Luis exchanged numbers and promised to keep in touch.

Before he walked out for good, Molly called out to him. He turned around and looked at her.

"Did your mom ever mention my mom?"

He thought for a moment.

"No, I'm sorry, I don't think she did."

"It's okay. I was just curious."

"By the way, and please don't take offense to this, but your sister is beautiful, even when she yacks."

"I'll be sure to let her know." Molly smiled.

After Luis left, Molly crawled into bed, curling up under the big down comforter, the air conditioning of the room keeping her cool while the down-feathers of the comforter kept her warm.

She could not wait to see what Letter #2 would bring, but she fell asleep much easier this time—even with Bennie's snoring.

CHAPTER TEN

For probably the first time in their lives, Molly woke up before Bennie. That's not to say it was early, though; it was ten in the morning. Like a child waiting for their parents to wake up on Christmas, Molly eagerly anticipated Bennie getting up.

Thirty minutes had passed, and Molly couldn't wait anymore. She got out of bed, walked over to where Bennie was still snoring, and lightly shook her.

"Bennie, wake up," she whispered.

Molly lightly shook her again.

"Hey, c'mon. Time to get up."

Bennie tossed a bit but didn't answer.

Molly shook her hard this time.

"Bennie!"

"What!?" Bennie yelled back, pulling the covers over her head.

"We have to read the next letter."

"It can wait," Bennie grumbled.

Molly sighed and rolled her eyes.

"I'm going to read it without you."

Bennie moaned and sat up. Last night's make-up was smeared down her face, and she smelled like leftover vodka.

"I feel like shit," Bennie said.

Molly laughed. "You look like it, too. Do you remember what happened last night?"

Bennie scowled, rubbing her temples with her fingers.

"No."

"Do you want me to tell you?"

"No."

"You were at the bar and—"

"I said no. God, this is horrible. How do you do this all the time?"

"I'm a professional. You just need to hone your skills." Molly smirked.

"Hand me my purse, please."

Molly grabbed Bennie's purse and handed it to her. Bennie reached in and pulled out a bottle of Advil.

"Can you get me some water?"

Molly grabbed one of the white foam cups meant for coffee, went into the bathroom, filled it with water from the sink, and handed Bennie the cup. Bennie popped a couple Advil into her mouth and chugged the cup of water.

"More," Bennie gasped, handing the empty cup back to Molly.

Molly huffed under her breath. Bennie was acting like a baby. She was hungover, not dying. Still, she took the cup and refilled it for her sister. Bennie chugged that cup, too.

"Thank you."

Molly sat down cross-legged on Bennie's bed with the envelope in her hands.

"Are you ready?" Molly asked excitedly.

"Hardly," Bennie said, one eye partially open, the other shut tight.

Molly opened the envelope and began to read out loud.

Hi girls!

Welcome to Letter #2! Did you enjoy Shirlington? Molly, did you stay out of trouble?

Molly laughed and looked at Bennie. Bennie didn't find it amusing.

I knew Luis would take good care of you. He knows Shirlington like the back of his hand and is familiar with all the neat places to see. His mom, Maria, and I were close friends. I bet I'm partying with her right now!

Molly felt like floating at the thought of Luis's mom and her dad laughing while watching their kids meet for the first time and run around Shirlington.

Shirlington was one of the first places I visited with your mom, but it wasn't the first time I had been there. The first time I went, I passed through for work and stopped at T&T for food. The second time I went to help fix T&T up. The third time I went, I brought your mom. It was the last time she would ever experience Shirlington.

I hope you were able to see Shirlington Park. That stream over there was always my favorite.

Anyway, are you girls ready for your next destination?

You're headed to Pylesville, Maryland, about a two-hour drive from Shirlington. This one is going to be a little bit tougher to figure out. I gave you an easy hint to get to Shirlington, but I'm going to challenge you a little more this time.

Your first clue is: Double silos

Your second clue is: Royalty

Love,

Dad

Molly put the letter down and looked at Bennie.

"Royalty."

"I feel nauseous," Bennie whined.

"Jesus. You need to eat something. Why don't we find somewhere to get food around here before we leave? We still have to walk back to where you parked the car."

"Ok. You're driving this time, though."

Molly laughed. "You got it."

They cleaned themselves up as much as they could. They had left their bags in the car, so they couldn't shower or change their clothes.

"I'm going to Google a place to eat," Bennie said.

"No, ma'am. Remember the rule!" Molly sang.

"I *really* don't care about your rule right now. I'm too hungover."

"Bennie, you're hungover, not dying. I thought you weren't a prude."

"I am. I am a prude, and I'm proud. So shut up. We can't all be impulsive and insane like you."

"Well, that was rude!" Molly put a hand defensively against her chest. She would typically take impulsive and insane as a compliment, but she knew Bennie wasn't using those words kindly.

"Truth hurts. Let's go."

The girls went downstairs and checked out of the hotel. They walked for a few minutes when they came across a diner. Molly read the name on the sign and gasped.

King's.

This one looked nothing like hers. It was a big, gray building with a beautiful outdoor patio with marble steps leading up to two glass doors.

Molly grabbed Bennie's arm, practically dragging her up the steps into the diner. The inside was just as pretty and inviting as the outside. Big red booths filled the entire restaurant, and bright ceiling lights shone down onto the patrons. Servers and busboys bustled from table to table.

The girls were seated at one of the big booths, the cushions nice and soft. A sweet, short blonde with a perfectly white smile took their orders. Molly sipped some coffee as they waited for their food.

"Are you excited to go to Maryland?" Molly asked.

"Yes, I just wish I wouldn't have had so much to drink last night," Bennie replied, avoiding eye contact.

"What's wrong?"

"It's just, I don't know. It's nothing."

"Doesn't sound like nothing. What's up?"

Usually, she didn't care to ask or hear about other people's woes. She had enough of her own. If someone told her it was nothing, then that's what it was—nothing.

But right now, it was just her and Bennie in a place they'd never been before, and they still had a long trip ahead of them, so if something was wrong, she figured she probably should know about it.

"Do you really care?"

Molly bit the inside of her cheek. She had that habit when she was nervous or felt off about something.

"I mean, yeah. Why wouldn't I?"

Bennie shrugged.

"I texted Tyler last night and told him I was drinking. Now, he's mad at me."

"He's *mad* at you? For what?"

"He asked who we met here, and I told him about Luis. The second he heard a guy's name, he got weird and distant."

Red flag.

"Later, I texted him and told him we were at Patty's. He asked if it was just you and me, and I was honest. When I told him Luis was there, he freaked out. He said being out at a bar with a guy was inappropriate when I had a boyfriend. I told him he was overreacting, and he hasn't answered me since."

Red flag.

"Is this the first time he's acted like this?"

"No. He gets really jealous and is just super insecure."

She must have seen the look of disgust on Molly's face.

"But he's working on it! He knows it's a problem. I just have to be a little patient with him."

"Hold on. So, our dad just died, and all Tyler is concerned about is if you keep that house and if you're out at a bar?"

"I—I don't know. But he is a really good guy! He's kind and funny, and he means well. He—"

As Bennie continued her defensive rant, trying to convince Molly that Tyler wasn't as awful as he seemed, Molly's eyes began to glaze. She was looking at Bennie, watching her mouth move, but she hadn't heard a single word coming out of her mouth.

"Hello?" Bennie asked, waving a hand in front of Molly's face.

Molly shook her head. "Yeah?"

"Oh my god, did you hear any of that?"

"Yes! I was listening! Tyler is a good guy, and he's funny."

Bennie rubbed her face with her hands. "Oh, my god. You really haven't changed. You didn't hear any of that."

"Yes, I did!"

"What was the last thing I said?" Bennie crossed her arms.

Molly gulped, searching for something to say. She glanced back and forth, then looked down, knowing she had been defeated.

"I'm sorry."

"Unreal. Forget about it."

They sat silently for a few minutes before Molly tried again to start a conversation that wouldn't bore her to death.

"Well, what about Luis?"

"What about him?"

"He seems like a really nice guy."

"He is a really nice guy."

"Do you like him?"

Bennie shifted in her seat and picked at her nails.

"No! I don't even know him. Not all of us run off with the first nice guy we meet."

"Maybe you should give it a try one day," Molly suggested, sipping her coffee.

"Yeah, maybe I should try taking your brilliant advice," Bennie sneered.

Ouch.

The sweet server returned with their food in time to interrupt before Molly snapped. The girls ate quietly but quickly. When they got their check, Bennie reached into her purse.

Her face turned white, and her eyes widened.

"What's wrong?"

"The money."

"What about it?"

"It's not in here."

"What?"

"It's not in here," Bennie frantically started pulling things out of her bag. "It's not in here! Oh my God, what are we going to do!?"

"Just hang on, okay? Let me think. Just let me think." Molly closed her eyes and took a deep breath.

Luckily Molly had some cash, but that wouldn't fix the fact that they were missing thousands of dollars. She thought hard about the last time she'd seen the envelope.

Patty's.

Bennie throwing up.

I grabbed the money.

The pissy bartender.

Fuck.

Molly paid the bill, and the girls left the diner. Molly immediately headed in the direction of Patty's.

"Where are we going?" Bennie asked, trying to keep up.

"Patty's."

Bennie froze. "I can't go back in there!"

Molly spun around and stared her sister down. "If you want to possibly get this money back, we have to go back in there."

"*You're* the one who lost it."

"How would you even know that? You were blacked out."

"Because you've barely said anything, you haven't immediately found someone else to blame, and you're headed right back to Patty's. I know you lost the money!" Bennie stomped her foot.

"You know what, you're right. I did. I did lose the money. And you acting like an overgrown toddler and vomiting all over the bar last night is the reason I lost it. Let's go."

"Oh my god, I vomited all over the bar?"

"Let's go!"

The entire walk to Patty's, Molly prayed for a different bartender. God either didn't have his listening ears on or flat-out ignored her pleas.

Patty's was much quieter at this time of day— they must have just opened. The bartender was wiping down the bar when he looked up and saw Molly and Bennie.

"Oh, hell no. Out. Both of you. Right now."

Molly put her hands up in submission. "Easy. Truce. We aren't here to drink. I think the sight of a vodka cranberry would throw this one into a downward spiral. I'm just checking to see if we forgot something here last night. Can you please help?"

Molly hadn't noticed last night, but the bartender was kind of cute. He had jet black hair that was slicked back, piercing blue eyes—similar to Jacey's—and clearly worked out.

"What did you leave?"

"It was a manilla envelope with— With some important stuff in it."

"Oh, this?" he squatted down, disappearing behind the bar for a moment, and then popped back up, envelope in hand.

"Yes! Oh my god, yes. Oh, thank God." Molly reached for the envelope, but the bartender snatched it back.

"I was stuck cleaning up *someone's* vomit last night." He looked past Molly and glared at Bennie.

"I'm really sorry about that." Bennie winced, scratching her head.

"So, why should I give this back to you?"

"Because it's ours," Molly said.

He dangled the envelope in the air, mocking them. "What's in it for me?" He smirked.

"Ew, dude, are you joking?" Molly said.

"I'm just saying I feel I'm owed something for my troubles."

"We don't owe you shit. I tipped you great last night. What is your problem? Never had someone throw up in a bar before?"

"No, my problem is entitled, rich tourists like you coming in and causing chaos," he hissed. "This envelope feels pretty heavy."

This guy was becoming increasingly less attractive the more he opened his mouth. Molly looked down at his name tag. *Harry*.

"Listen, I'm sorry your parents hate you and gave you a horrible name like Harry. That isn't my fault. Now give me the envelope."

"No."

Molly couldn't believe what she was hearing. There was no way this guy was being such a dick about a drunk girl throwing up.

"I'm really sorry for last night!" Bennie finally called from behind Molly. "I don't usually drink, and I was fighting with my boyfriend. If we could please just have the envelope back, we'd appreciate it." She smiled innocently.

"And I'd appreciate it if stupid bitches like y—"

"Okay!" Molly clapped her hands together. "I'm done with this."

She hoisted herself up onto the bar and jumped over. Harry's eyes widened. A few female servers were starting to come out to see what the commotion was.

"Molly, stop!" Bennie screamed, covering her ears with her hands and shutting her eyes tight.

"Get out from behind the bar!" he yelled.

Molly cocked back and punched Harry right in his nose, sending him tumbling to the floor, the envelope falling out of his hand.

"Molly!" Bennie screamed again.

"What the fuck!?" Harry moaned in pain.

Molly looked back at Bennie. "Run!"

Bennie ran, still covering her ears, and Molly grabbed the envelope off the floor. She looked at Harry, lying in a fetal position, covering his nose with his hands, blood pouring between his fingers. She grabbed his rag from the bar and knelt down next to him. She turned him over onto his back and grabbed the collar of his shirt, leaning in close to whisper in his ear.

"Call the cops. I would love to see it. I'm sure they'd be interested in hearing how you tried to use unsolicited advances to give a patron their belongings back and how you called my sister a bitch."

Harry groaned again but said nothing.

"I know your type. You're a good-looking guy. Well, you were, before the broken nose and all. I'm sure girls leave their numbers for you on their receipts. I'm sure you've used that on other girls, and it's worked, right?"

Harry was silent. Molly grabbed his jaw and turned him, so his face was adjacent to hers. Harry yelped.

"I said, 'right?'"

Harry nodded.

"Well, wrong girls, you piece of shit. You might be hot, but you're just a sad college dropout who still lives at home with mom and dad. And I can guarantee you, every female server in this bar knows it, too. That's why the cops aren't here yet, right?"

"Just leave me alone, please. This is too far."

Molly tensed, stood up and took a step back. Harry's eyes were already starting to bruise, which meant she'd definitely broken his nose. She started to feel sorry for him. Maybe she didn't have to leap over the bar. Maybe she could have gotten a manager or called the cops.

She glanced around the room and saw three female servers standing in silent awe. No one said a word, but the looks on their faces confirmed precisely what Molly was thinking, and suddenly her concerns disappeared.

That motherfucker had it coming.

Molly looked back down at Harry. Good thing he wasn't a bouncer because one hit to the nose and he was still on the ground. His blood had poured all over the floor. Molly grabbed a rag from the bar and tossed it at him.

"Here. You have another mess to clean up."

Molly walked out of the bar to see Bennie sitting on the pavement outside, hugging her knees, shaking.

"Are you okay?"

Bennie stared straight ahead. "Yeah, I'm okay. Are you okay?"

Molly's right hand throbbed. The adrenaline was starting to wear off. She stretched her fingers, then shook her hand in the air. "My hand hurts a little, but his nose definitely hurts worse."

"I shouldn't have run. I should have stayed. He could have hurt you."

Molly reached her arm out to help Bennie stand up.

"Don't worry about it. C'mon, Maryland awaits."

"Excuse me?" A small, squeaky voice came from around the corner. It was one of the servers.

"Yeah?" Molly stood up straight, unsure of what to expect.

"I just wanted to tell you…that was awesome. Harry is a nightmare. We'll have your back if he tries anything, which I doubt he will."

"Thank you."

The girls walked back to the parked car. They grabbed their bags and changed into new clothes in the back seat. Once they were settled, Molly took the spot in the driver's seat, put the key in the ignition, and started the car.

"You ready?" she asked.

"I am."

Molly put Pylesville, Maryland, in her GPS— two hours and fifteen minutes. She played music, and both girls sat quietly for a few minutes.

"Why did you hit him?"

Molly looked over at Bennie, then down at her hand, which was starting to bruise. She stretched her fingers again, the pain shooting to her fingertips. She hoped it wasn't broken. She lifted her sunglasses from her face, pushing back her curls.

"He had our money, and he was a douchebag."

Bennie nodded.

"And he called you a bitch."

Bennie smiled and soon after fell asleep. *Poor thing. She needs to sleep off the rest of last night.*

As they drove, Molly's phone played music softly through the car. Her phone pinged, and she saw the same number from yesterday.

Hey. It's me again. I just wanted to see if you got my last text.

"Just answer him," Bennie said, her eyes still closed.

Molly jumped. "I thought you were asleep."

Bennie opened her eyes slightly and looked over at Molly.

"Are you going to tell me the truth about what happened?"

"Do you know something?"

"No, other than I've gotten pretty good at figuring out when you're lying."

"We broke up."

"Why?" Bennie sat up in her seat, opening her eyes fully.

"It's really hard to explain."

"Have you talked to anyone about it?"

"Yes. No. Kind of. I don't really have many friends anymore," Molly bit the inside of her cheek. "It's really just Jacey."

"Who's Jacey?"

"My only friend."

Bennie smiled sympathetically and put a hand on Molly's shoulder.

"I'm your friend, too."

"Thanks. I really don't know how to respond to his texts. It's just so random for him to suddenly want to talk to me."

"If I had to guess, it's probably because our dad just passed away, and he's human with normal emotions, like empathy. Text him back. See what he wants."

Molly sighed and looked at her phone. The text from Liam was still on the screen. She picked the phone up and began typing.

Hey. Yeah, I got it. Can I call you tonight?

Within seconds her phone pinged again.

Absolutely.

Bennie grinned, looking out of the passenger window.

"What?" Molly asked.

Bennie turned and looked at Molly, the grin never leaving her face.

"I'm so proud of you."

CHAPTER ELEVEN

Once off the highway, Molly admired the ride through Maryland. Winding roads lined with trees, farms, and horses calmly grazing reminded her a bit of home. The biggest difference was the houses, which were few and far between but gorgeous. Some were newer mansions with long paved driveways and acres of green fields, and some were older farmhouses, but each one was as stunning as the last.

Molly drove aimlessly, exploring. The girls oohed and aahed at each home they passed, making up stories about what they thought the families living there were like, or what they did for a living. They eagerly pointed out every horse, deer, and little animal they saw.

"So, Luis was nice!" Molly said, straying away from their discussion of imaginary families.

"You said that already." Bennie rolled her eyes. "But yes, he was. I can't believe he carried me all the way back to the hotel."

"He said you were beautiful, by the way."

"He did not." Bennie's pale cheeks turned rosy red.

"He did, and you're blushing! Have you heard from Tyler?"

"Nope. I tried texting him again this morning, but he never answered."

"Do you want Luis's number?"

"No! Tyler's just in a mood. He'll be fine soon."

Molly decided to drop the topic of Luis and continued to look around for what "royalty" and "double silos" could mean. There were silos everywhere; how was she supposed to know which ones her dad was referring to? She drove a few more miles and saw a dirt parking lot on the side of the road. She pulled in and saw an entrance to a hiking trail.

"Did you figure it out?" Bennie asked.

"No, but I need to stretch my legs, and there's a hiking trail right here. I figured we could at least check it out."

The girls got out of the car and were met with fresh air and a slight breeze. The sun beamed through the tree leaves, gently warming their faces.

They began walking through the trail entrance, which consisted of a ton of large rocks and dirt. They crossed over a small wooden bridge that overlooked a tiny stream. Molly looked down into the stream and saw tiny minnows swimming by.

As they walked, Molly heard heavy water flowing in the distance. She stopped abruptly to listen, making Bennie stumble into her.

"Ow, what the hell?"

"Shhh. Do you hear that?" Molly asked.

Bennie listened closely and shook her head.

"I think it's a waterfall."

As they walked, they could either continue uphill on the trail or cross over the stream on rocks to get to a different trail. The sound of the waterfall was getting louder, and Molly was determined to find it.

"I'm going to walk up there and see where it takes me."

Bennie, who was taking pictures with her phone, nodded.

"I'm going to take a couple more pictures down here; this is gorgeous!"

Molly trekked up the rocky hill until she got to the top, realizing there was nothing up there but the edge of a cliff. She walked to the tip of it and looked around. To her left, she could see the rocks that made the way to the trail on the other side of the stream and

Bennie bending down, trying to get the perfect angle for her pictures.

To the right, she could almost see a full view of the waterfall. From where she stood, she could see they'd have to cross over the stream to get right in front of it. She quickly returned to Bennie, ran up behind her, and grabbed her shoulders.

"We have to cross the stream to get to the waterfall!"

"I don't know if I trust walking over those rocks."

"Why?"

"I don't want to fall in the water."

"It's three feet deep. I think you'll be okay."

The memory of the kayak came to Molly's mind. She scratched her head as if trying to scratch the memory away.

"C'mon, I'll help you."

Molly and Bennie got to the line of rocks, the stream water flowing through the gaps quickly. Molly stepped onto the first rock, turned around, and reached for Bennie's hand.

"Nice and slow. We're in no rush!"

Bennie took a deep breath, grabbed Molly's hand and slowly stuck out her left foot. She balanced herself and paused, one foot on the rock, the other still on land.

"I can't do this." Bennie started to panic.

"You can! You're already a quarter of the way there. I got you!" She gently shook their locked hands in the air.

Bennie took another deep breath and moved her other leg from the land. Finally, she had both feet on the first rock and focused fiercely on balancing.

"See!? Good job! Now we're going to the second rock."

They repeated this several times, Molly talking to Bennie the entire way. They were going painfully slow for Molly's liking, but she kept her patience. Rock by rock, they crossed until they had reached the other side. Once they did, the girls celebrated and cheered.

Bennie saw the waterfall and gasped. "You were right! It is a waterfall, and it's so pretty!"

Molly turned and looked behind her. She could see the top of the waterfall, but giant boulders blocked the full view. They walked over and climbed up each boulder, one by one, until they reached the top. They stood quietly, hypnotized by the waterfall's beauty. It poured gracefully to the bottom, creating the pool that'd started the stream.

Bennie nudged Molly. "You know what I've always wanted to do?"

"What's that?"

Bennie went to the lower part of the rocks. Molly watched in shock as her sister kicked her shoes off and leaped into the water, landing on her feet in the knee-deep water. She ran under the waterfall and stood beneath it, lifting her arms in the air, tilting her head back towards the sky, and laughing.

"It's f-f-freezing!"

Five minutes earlier, Bennie hadn't wanted to cross a shallow stream. Now here she was, fully clothed, standing under a waterfall.

Molly had never felt more proud.

Molly followed Bennie's lead. The water was indeed freezing cold but also refreshing. She tried to focus on each drop as it touched her skin. She imagined the water washing away every wrong she had ever done.

They both stood, letting the moment of happiness thrive, smiling towards the sky. The thundering sound of the water rushing over them made hearing anything else nearly impossible.

"Bennie!"

Bennie twirled in blissful ignorance.

"Love you," Molly whispered.

Once they were done, they got out of the water and started the walk back. When they had reached the stream to cross back over, Molly offered her hand to Bennie. Bennie looked herself up and down, her shorts and t-shirt sopping wet.

"I think I'll be fine this time," she laughed.

She crossed over the rocks without any help from Molly. As they arrived at the dirt parking lot, Bennie stopped at the wooden information board while Molly continued walking to the car.

"It says we're in Rock State Park! Apparently, that waterfall is called Kilgore Falls!"

Molly, once again changing her clothes in the back seat of the car, gave Bennie a thumbs up.

"This park is so much bigger than I thought it was!"

"That's cool!" Molly yelled back, only half paying attention.

"Oh my God, Molly, come over here! Quick!"

"Jesus Christ, what do you want?" Molly murmured.

She looked out the rear window to see her sister jumping up and down, pointing at something on the information board. She sighed, threw a new shirt on and got out of the car.

"Look!" Bennie said, pointing at a map on the information board. "King and Queen Seat. *Royalty*. I don't know what the King and Queen seat is, but I bet that's what Dad meant when he said royalty!"

Molly smiled, impressed by her sister's detective work. Then she remembered the other clue. *Double silos.* Not wanting to ruin Bennie's excitement, Molly stayed positive but realistic.

"Good job! We can check it out. We just need to figure out what he meant by 'double silos.'"

Bennie pursed her lips and held a pointer finger to them, thinking. Molly knew Bennie was determined to figure this one out, especially since Molly had figured out where they needed to be so quickly in Shirlington.

"Well, he said in the first letter that there would be a person or people who knew we would be coming; they just don't know when. This place on the map is in a state park, and I doubt someone has just been waiting for us to show up. So, it has to be a different location." Bennie squinted her eyes and scratched her head.

"Maybe we just keep driving? I feel like, eventually, we'll see something that sticks out."

Bennie nodded, and the two left the dirt parking lot, hoping for a miracle. Driving through the winding roads and passing the farms and horses again, there were silos every few miles. Molly knew her dad said this would be hard, but she couldn't imagine him making his daughters knock on strangers' doors or trekking through random farms.

Molly's phone pinged, and she looked down, hoping it wasn't Liam again. Thankfully it was Luis.

Are you having fun!? Where did the next letter take you? And how is Bennie feeling?

Molly began typing back.

We are! We're in Maryland. We haven't found the next letter yet. Bennie is fine. A little hungover, but it seems to be wearing off. Thanks for helping her last night. :)

"Who's that?"

"It's Luis. He's just checking in."

"Oh," Bennie tucked a piece of hair behind her ear and cleared her throat. "That was very kind of him."

They drove until they passed a golf course with green hills and flats. Molly squinted and saw what looked like a restaurant in the distance. Her stomach gurgled. She slowed down as they got closer.

"What are you doing?"

"I'm starving."

"Molly, are you kidding me?"

"I'm sorry! I just need something quick."

She hadn't paid much attention to the restaurant or what it looked like when she'd pulled in, distracted by hunger. She parked the car and began gathering her things when Bennie smacked her in the arm.

"Ow! What!?"

Bennie pointed at the restaurant.

It was an older, gray building. To the left in the parking lot was an old, green John Deere tractor with yellow tires. The restaurant was surrounded by the green of the golf course. The entrance was covered by a red awning that read "Geneva Farm Golf Club," on each side of the building were identical silos.

"There's no way this is it," Molly said, shaking her head in disbelief.

"We won't know until we get inside!" Bennie giggled.

They hurried inside the restaurant. When they first entered, a blue and gray sign read "Twin Silos." The girls looked at each other in shock, but it was starting to seem more likely that they were in the right place.

Twin Silo's had clearly once been a barn with tall, wood-paneled ceilings. There were windows on every wall that peered out to the golf course. Two doors in the back had once been barn doors—their panels painted blue, with a blue piece of wood crossing over them to ensure no one tried to open them.

A whiteboard at the front read, "Please Seat Yourself!" with a smiley face. To the right was a small bar, and throughout the restaurant were tables and chairs.

Molly and Bennie sat down at the bar. An older, blonde bartender with pigtails in her hair greeted them with menus.

"Hi, girls! What can I get started for ya' today?"

"I'll just have water, please," Bennie said.

"I'll do the same, and the cream of crab soup, please."

The bartender nodded and began pouring them some water. Molly decided to take a shot in the dark.

"I'm sorry; I don't mean to bother you. But did you happen to know a Michael Thurman?"

The bartender stopped pouring and slowly pushed the water across the bar toward Molly.

"Why do you ask?" She raised an eyebrow.

"Well, he's our dad and unfor—"

"Oh my god, you're here!" the bartender shrieked, throwing herself across the bar at Molly and wrapping her arms around Molly's neck. She then did the same to Bennie.

"Oh, girls, I am so sorry for your loss. But I'm so happy to finally meet you!"

"Are you the one with the next letter?" Bennie asked.

"Oh god, no! But things don't stay a secret for very long in this little bar." She winked. "I'm Suzanne. It's so nice to meet you both! I know exactly who to put you in touch with." She leaned in close and covered her face with her hand. "Do you see that gentleman over there?"

An older man sat alone at the end of the bar. He was wearing a flat cap, slacks, and a white, short-sleeved shirt, sipping what looked like a soda. The girls nodded.

"His name's Eddie. That's who you want to talk to."

"Thank you," Molly said.

The girls took their water and went down to where Eddie sat. Before they got there, Molly pulled Bennie to the side.

"Do you want to take this one?" she asked, her voice lowered.

"What do I say?"

"I don't know, just introduce us as Michael's daughters. With how Suzanne acted, it seems like Dad was well known."

Bennie rubbed the back of her neck. "I don't know, Moll."

"I'll do it; I just figured you'd want to—"

"No, it's okay. I got this."

The two approached Eddie, and Bennie lightly tapped him on his shoulder. He turned around and looked them over.

"Hi, ladies," he said, smiling.

"Hi, um, my name is Bennie."

A long pause.

"Mhm?" Eddie raised his grey, furry eyebrows, waiting for Bennie to go on.

"And this is my sister, um, Molly."

Molly waved.

"A pleasure to meet you two," Eddie said, removing his cap to reveal a mostly bald head.

"We're Michael's daughters. Um, do you- do you know Michael?" Bennie uttered.

Eddie rubbed his chin. "I'm sorry, I don't believe that I do."

Bennie froze, the color from her already pale face somehow fading even more.

"Oh, oh jeez. Okay, um, I am so sorry. I'm really sorry to bother you. Please just ignore us. It's silly. We were just—We thought— The waitress told us that—"

Eddie flashed a wicked grin. "I'm kidding. Yes, I know your dad quite well."

Bennie exhaled loudly, her body slumping against one of the empty chairs. Molly laughed obnoxiously.

"Come on, join me outside. I need a cigarette."

The girls followed Eddie outside. He sat down in one of the rocking chairs and offered a cigarette to each of them. Bennie declined, but Molly took one and put it to her mouth. Eddie lit it for her with an old, rusty zippo.

"I'm very sorry to hear about your dad," Eddie said, taking a drag from the cigarette. As he spoke, clouds of smoke followed his words. "He really was a great man. It was rare to meet someone with the same craving for adventure as me! He was one of a kind!"

The girls thanked him for his condolences.

"So, tell me about your adventure so far." Eddie's eyes sparkled like he had been holding on to a secret he finally had permission to tell.

The girls told him about Shirlington, meeting Luis, the tacos, and their experience in the city. Eddie wanted every detail, asking questions and digging when he felt he hadn't gotten the entire story. Molly had tried to dull down the story of her punching the bartender, but Eddie wouldn't allow it. When he heard the whole story, he went into a fit of laughter so strong he had to hold his stomach.

"What about you, Eddie? Do you have any stories?" Bennie asked.

Eddie's face lit up. "Well, I was a park ranger for sixty years. I'm retired now, but I worked at parks all over—Canada, New Hampshire, Maine, Wyoming. I even visited New Zealand once! That was my favorite. They had dog bowls full of beer for the working dogs tied up outside while their owners drank beer inside. Pretty damn funny to see."

The girls listened intently. Eddie was animated, which made him a good storyteller, and they were captivated by him as he talked about his travels. They sat in awe as they heard about all of the life he had lived and everywhere he'd been.

"How did you meet our Dad?" Molly asked.

Eddie chuckled. "I met your dad and your mom when they were still in college. They pulled up here at

Twin Silos to grab something to eat. I was outside and overheard them trying to find the best views."

He took a sip of his drink and cleared his throat.

"I kind of helped myself to their conversation and asked if I could make a recommendation. They were interested, so I took a piece of receipt paper, drew a quick map for them, and your dad bought me a drink. I'm a Quaker, ya' know, but some people confuse us for Mennonites. We're not. We drink, and we drive." He laughed.

"Anyway, we talked for a little while before they headed out to go see the views. They came back two hours later, and your mom was flashing a big ol' diamond rock on her left hand. Your dad thanked me for making it the best proposal ever. I had no idea that was even his plan."

He took another drag of his cigarette.

"After that, he would come back to visit every so often and make me tell more of my stories. He never got bored of them. He stopped coming here after a while, though, and I always wondered what happened to him."

Eddie paused for a moment, his face sulking.

"To my surprise, a few months ago, he walked in here again to give me the letter for you girls and told me why he hadn't been around."

Eddie's eyes fogged, and he wiped them with his finger, then quickly shook it off. Eddie reached into his wallet, pulled out a folded-up piece of receipt paper, and handed it to Molly. On it was a map scribbled in black pen with directions to a circled location.

The King and Queen Seat.

"Take this. Your dad gave it back to me the same day he came and gave me the letter. Oh! Speaking of which—come on!"

He put his cigarette out in a bucket of sand, and the girls followed him back into Twin Silos. Molly's soup awaited her, and she eagerly scooped a spoonful into her mouth. *Nothing better than crab soup from Maryland.*

Eric called out to Suzanne.

"Yes, my dear?" Suzanne sang, resting her elbow on the bar and chin on her hand.

"Can you go into the cash register and lift the till up? There's an envelope in there."

Suzanne nodded and came back with the envelope.

"I'm sure you girls are aware of the rules by now, right?"

Molly and Bennie nodded in unison.

"Perfect. Oh, and hang on!"

Eddie reached across the bar, grabbed a pen and a napkin, and wrote two addresses.

"The first address is to a really great winery that you can check out. The second one is my home. My wife and I have two spare bedrooms you can use. Feel free to crash if you'd like. I told your dad I would keep you safe. Matter of fact, I'll hold on to this letter until you're back."

"Thank you so much, Eddie," Molly said. "We honestly didn't know how to find a place with double silos or what that even meant. It was really a coincidence that we ended up here."

Eddie took another sip of his drink and smiled. "A wise person once said, 'There's no such thing as a coincidence in this world. What does exist is only the inevitable.'"

CHAPTER TWELVE

The sisters followed Eddie's hand-drawn map through more winding roads. Molly couldn't help but laugh at the thought of following a receipt, but she traced the lines with her finger as she navigated for Bennie.

As they trekked on, Molly noticed that the road had started to steepen, and soon they were rounding the corners of a mountain. She looked down as they passed by a river, watching people on kayaks paddling through the water. It reminded Molly of her first plane ride to Disney World. She had fought with Bennie for the window seat, and after some arguing, their dad intervened.

"Bennie, just let Molly have the window seat, please," Michael said, exasperated. "You can have it on the way home, I promise."

Bennie pouted but sat in the middle seat while Molly basked in her victory, looking out the window as the plane ascended. She noticed that the higher they went, the smaller everything looked. She imagined reaching down and picking up the buses, cars, and people like tiny toys until finally, all she could see was blue sky and clouds.

She wondered why her dad had sided with her so quickly. Looking back on it, she realized he likely knew it would be easier for Bennie to oblige than Molly.

They continued to climb the curving road until they saw a brown wooden sign showing the way to the King and Queen Seat. They pulled into the gravel parking lot, but they couldn't see much from where they were. There was a small, old, rusty playground in front of them where a couple of teenagers stood around, a trash can, a path, and some trees. Molly wondered if they were in the right place, but the sign pointed towards the path.

"Is this really it?" Bennie asked.

"Let's walk down and find out, I guess."

A large sign along the path read:

USE CAUTION. LARGE DROPS. DEATHS HAVE OCCURRED. NO SMALL CHILDREN OR PETS.

Bennie's eyes were wide with worry.

They continued to walk when Molly saw a small brown sign to her left and stopped to read it.

"What's it say?" Bennie asked, picking at her nails again.

"Nothing bad, just some history," Molly said, glancing over the sign.

"So, what does it say?" Bennie asked suspiciously.

Molly sighed and read out loud.

"Rock State Park: The King and Queen Seat. The King and Queen Seat to your right is a natural 190-foot rock outcrop that overlooks Deer Creek Valley. This cliff affords a spectacular view of Harford County's rolling hills and farmland."

Molly looked down the path and to the right. She could see the King and Queen Seat.

"Made of quartzite and a hard quartz-pebble meta— Metacon— Metacon—"

Bennie looked over her shoulder. "Metaconglomerate."

"Whatever, the King and Queen Seat was formed millions of years ago when quartz was subjected to intense heat and pressure. The surrounding ancient rocks eroded away, leaving a tall 'tower' of rock. In 1879, Thomas Wysong published *The Rocks of Deer Creek*, where he confessed to 'intermingling fact and fancy.' According to Wysong, during the 1680s, local

Susquehannock Indians used the King and Queen Seat as a site for ceremonial gatherings. Tribal Chief Bald Eagle and his wife sat upon the King and Queen Seat while braves gathered below to listen to orators. Wysong claimed that from this spot, Bald Eagle and his wife witnessed their son, Bird-That-Flies-High, wed the Iroquois maiden, Fern-Shaken-By-The-Wind. No evidence has surfaced to support Wysong's account."

"That would be amazing if he was telling the truth!" Bennie said.

"For centuries, the Rocks at Deer Creek were a popular site-seeing and picnicking destination. To ensure the King and Queen Seat's preservation, the State of Maryland purchased the site in 1949. Rocks State Park opened two years later."

"That's actually incredible," Bennie said softly.

They continued walking. The dirt and leaves under their feet crunched until they reached smaller boulders they had to climb, the smaller boulders turned into larger boulders, and the larger boulders turned into a long, flat, pointed cliff edge. Molly slowly and carefully led the way as they neared the edge.

Standing beside each other at one hundred and ninety feet above the ground, they looked out. Summer shades of green were everywhere across the farmlands. The horses, farms, and silos looked so small from where they stood.

The wind whipped through Molly's hair as she imagined what this place must have been like centuries ago. She imagined an Indian Chief and his wife sitting on the "throne," watching their son be wed. She imagined thousands of people gathering below to hear stories like she and Bennie had listened to Eddie's. She imagined her father proposing to her mother.

Bennie's eyes watered.

"What's wrong?" Molly asked.

Two tears fell down her cheek, and she wiped

them away.

"This is just so beautiful. I remember a little bit

more about Mom than you do. I think Dad proposing

here is incredible and—"

More tears fell down Bennie's cheeks, and Molly

instinctively wrapped her arms around her.

"I just miss him so much," Bennie sobbed.

"Me, too, Ben. Me, too."

Molly let go of Bennie, sat, and patted the

ground beside her. Their legs dangled over the edge.

"He just really set the bar high for my

expectations in men." Bennie giggled, then sniffled.

"Well, does Tyler meet those?"

Bennie was quiet for a moment, sniffling again

before she responded. "I don't know."

"Luis asked about you." Molly said.

Bennie perked up a bit, wiping her eyes, mascara running down her face. "Did he?"

"He did." Molly wiped the mascara from under Bennie's eyes. "He asked how you were feeling. I told him you were fine and thanked him again for helping to get you to the hotel."

"It was very nice of him. And don't get me wrong, he's a good-looking guy, but I love Tyler."

"Why?"

Bennie was quiet again. She looked up, as if searching through the filing cabinets in her brain for a decent answer.

"I-I don't know."

"How did Dad feel about Tyler?"

Bennie let out a belly-laugh. "Remember how he felt about Liam?"

"Yeah."

"Yeah. He felt just as great about Tyler, too. So don't feel like you were the only one he harped on about boyfriends."

The girls sat on the cliff edge for a few hours. They talked about boys, their dad, and growing up. They reminisced on childhood and what they thought their lives would've been versus how they turned out.

"I'm sorry if it always seemed like I was trying to be your mom. I felt like I had to since you didn't really get to have one. I felt like it was unfair for you."

"I get that now. And for what it's worth, you did a great job."

Bennie looked at Molly, obviously waiting for more.

Molly rolled her eyes. "And I'm sorry for being such a bitch sometimes."

Bennie grinned, appeased. "Thank you."

"And I'm sorry I didn't let you have the window seat?"

"What?"

"That one time on our way to Disney. We fought over the window seat. I'm sorry. I should have let you have it."

"Molly, you were like, seven. Who cares?"

"I do. I'm sorry."

Bennie blinked hard. "It's— It's fine."

The sundown skies were starting to roll, and it would be dark in no time.

"You want to go check out that winery Eddie was telling us about?" Molly asked.

"Yeah, sure. Let's go."

The two got up and began climbing back over boulders, making their way through the trail until they reached the parking lot again.

They pulled into Harford Winery and parked with hundreds of other cars on the grass.

It was much more modern than Twin Silos. The walls were painted grey, and the décor was rustic. There was a small gift shop with cute signs, t-shirts and small home décor. Almost every table was full of people, chatting and laughing, sipping wine. At the front was a small desk with paper menus and pencils. Another sweet, bubbly blonde woman stood behind the desk with a warm, welcoming smile.

"Hi, ladies! Welcome! Have we been here before?"

The girls shook their heads.

"Well, welcome! You can grab a paper menu and a pencil and circle whichever wine you'd like. Flights are ten dollars for six, or you can buy by the glass or bottle."

Molly was impressed that no one seemed *drunk*. One lady was even holding a baby. These were the kind of people who really had their shit figured out.

She decided to try some dry white wines, and Bennie opted for the sweet white wines. They handed the menus back to the woman at the desk.

"I'll bring these right out! You can sit wherever you'd like."

Molly bought some cheese and crackers, and the girls found a table.

"My name's Beth," she said, placing the trays that held the flights down in front of the girls. "I'll be helping you tonight. Please let me know if you have any questions!"

"Thanks, Beth!" Molly said.

Beth winked and then checked on a few other guests, laughing and talking with everyone as if she'd known them her whole life.

The girls took sips from each of their taster cups, discussing which ones they loved, which were okay, and which they hated. They passed the small cups back and forth to each other.

Beth returned to the table and put a hand on each of their shoulders.

"Did we want to try another flight?"

"I think we're going to get a glass of the Rosewood, please," Bennie said.

"Yes! That's my favorite, too! Good choice!" Beth gave a thumbs up.

Even though Beth was older than the girls, she was trendy. She wore a form-fitting black shirt with blue skinny jeans, ripped in the knees. Her bleach blonde hair was neatly curled, and her make-up was nicely done. Molly aspired to be like that when she was older.

Beth came back with two glasses of Rosewood. Bennie's phone pinged, and she squinted.

"Who is it?" Molly asked.

"I don't know; I don't have the number saved."
Bennie's jaw dropped.

"What? Who is it?"

Bennie stared blankly at her phone.

Molly's gut twisted. Something was wrong.
Even Beth had stopped and waited, either in concern or
nosiness. Bennie showed Molly the screen. It was a
picture of a pretty girl with long brown hair lying in bed,
smiling.

Tyler was asleep next to her.

"What the f—" Molly tried to scream, but
Bennie quickly covered her mouth.

"Shut. Up."

"Is everything okay?" Beth asked.

"No!" Molly yelled, the wine starting to show.
"My sister's douchebag boyfriend hasn't answered her in

almost two days, and she just got a picture of him sleeping next to some girl!"

"What!?" Beth yelled. She grabbed a chair, pulled it up next to Bennie, and listened intently.

"Thanks." Bennie glared at Molly.

"Are you okay? Do you want me to kill him?" Beth asked, rubbing Bennie's shoulder.

"I'm okay, I think. I don't know. I'm just really shocked." Bennie's eyes welled with tears.

"Oh honey, no, no, no, no. No tears!" Beth said, wiping Bennie's cheek.

"I just can't believe it. That girl— That girl is Grace's mom."

"Give me your phone," Molly demanded.

"Absolutely not," Bennie said.

"Right now."

"Well, hang on a second," Beth intervened, trying to mediate. "Let her process this."

"To think he was the one questioning *me* last night is insane."

"There ya' go, honey. Get mad!" Beth encouraged.

"I've been nothing but loyal, and loving, and caring, and this is what he does!?"

"Disgusting!" Beth egged on.

"I've been gone for two days! Two *fucking* days!"

"And he has the nerve!?"

Molly saw what Beth was doing. It was one of Molly's favorite tricks. Turn your sadness into anger so you're not sad; you're just *pissed*.

"And talk about timing; my *dad* just died. And I *found him* dead. And this piece of shit tries to act all sweet, and caring, and concerned. But all he wanted was *my dad's house.*"

"He's the worst!" Beth yelled.

"Yeah, he is!" Molly encouraged.

"He's the worst!" Bennie screamed.

"He's the worst. He's the worst. He's the worst," Beth chanted, standing up and raising her arms to encourage the rest of the crowd to join in.

Molly stood and started chanting, too, but throwing her own spin on it.

"Fuck, Ty-ler. Fuck, Ty-ler. Fuck, Ty-ler!"

Soon another person started chanting, then another, then another, until the entire winery was either chanting "Fuck, Ty-ler" or "He's the worst".

Molly gleamed. Maybe these people didn't have it all together like she'd thought.

Bennie downed the glass of wine, and everyone cheered as she chugged. She swallowed hard, wiped her mouth, grabbed the envelope from her purse, and threw down cash.

"Let's go," she said to Molly, slamming the glass on the table and walking towards the door.

Molly stood to follow. Before she left, she turned to Beth.

Thank you, she mouthed.

Beth waved at her and winked.

Bennie was already in the car's passenger seat by the time Molly caught up with her. She was texting furiously, her fingers a blur. Molly got into the car.

"You okay?"

"I will be." Her tears were gone. Her pupils were so large, her eyes looked black.

"Honestly, he kind of sucked anyway." Molly cringed.

"I don't have time for you to tell me you told me so," Bennie snapped. "Send me Luis's phone number."

Molly sent Bennie Luis's phone number, took a deep breath, and then typed in the address to Eddie's house—ten minutes.

Eddie's house was one of the cute, quaint farm homes. It had white wood siding and a small front porch with an awning. Two rocking chairs with chipping paint creaked back and forth in the breeze. Molly and Bennie grabbed their bags from the car, walked up the steps to the front door and knocked.

Suzanne from Twin Silo's opened the door, and Molly jumped slightly.

"Oh, good! I am so glad you made it!"

Molly cocked her head to the side, trying to figure out why Suzanne was at Eddie's house. *Did he give me the wrong address?* Suzanne didn't seem to notice Molly's confusion.

"Please, come in! Sit down and get comfy! I'll grab Eddie." Suzanne shuffled to the kitchen.

The inside of the house was just as vintage-country-like as the outside. Tan wallpaper with small flowers covered the walls of the living room. The floors were made of natural wood, and a couple of deer heads were on the wall. It was outdated, but Molly admired its charm.

Eddie came out of the kitchen, wiping his hands on his jeans. Before he could say a word, Bennie spoke up.

"I don't mean to be rude, but I think the wine gave me a headache. Is it okay if I just go lay down?"

"Absolutely! Suzanne, can you please show Bennie the spare bedroom?"

Suzanne motioned for Bennie to follow her, and the two went upstairs.

"Are you guys friends?" Molly asked.

"Who? Me and Suzanne?" He let out a laugh. "We're married!"

"Oh! Oh, wow. I— I'm sorry! I j-just wasn't s-sure."

"I know; she's out of my league." Eddie grinned.

Molly shook her head and smiled back. Eddie went to the kitchen and came back with water. Molly thanked him and took a sip. Suzanne came back downstairs, visibly upset.

"What's the matter?" Eddie asked.

"Bennie just told me what happened tonight," Suzanne said, looking at Molly.

"Yeah, rough night."

"Infidelity," Suzanne tried to whisper to Eddie.

Eddie raised his eyebrows. "Oh, no. Poor girl."

"We've all been there. Bastards," Suzanne said.

"It's so weird, too, because Bennie and I talked about him earlier today and how she wasn't sure why she loved him. I kind of insinuated that he was wasn't all that great. Hours later, we find this out. It's just a weird coincide—"

"There's no such thing as a coincidence in this world," Eddie started.

"What does exist is only the inevitable." She gave Eddie a knowing look.

The pain in Bennie's face—the anger and betrayal in her voice—ignited something in Molly's memory. She shifted in her chair.

"I'm so sorry, but I'm sure you understand that we're just exhausted after the last few days. Could I see myself up to my room?" Molly asked.

"Of course. Are you sure you don't want me to walk you up?" Suzanne asked.

"I'm sure. Thank you."

She went upstairs and saw three bedrooms, one with the door shut. She opened it slightly and could see the shadow of Bennie lying on the bed, the phone screen's light slightly lighting up the room.

"You okay?"

Bennie turned over. "Yeah, I'm okay. Just texting Luis."

"Okay, just checking. Love you."

"Love you, too."

Molly shut Bennie's door and found the other spare bedroom. She quietly locked her door, then grabbed her phone.

She held the phone up to her ear as it rang. Her heart pounded; her stomach turned.

"Hello?"

"Hey. It's me."

CHAPTER THIRTEEN

When Molly was ten, she accidentally hit Bennie in the head with a softball during a game of catch. Bennie cried, and when their dad came rushing out, he told Molly to apologize. Instead, Molly ran inside, grabbed an ice pack, and returned to hold it to her sister's head.

"Pay attention next time," was all she could say.

She crashed her dad's car into a telephone pole while texting when she was seventeen.

"I'll pay for the damages."

Molly always felt like actions were better than words. What does an apology mean without corrected behavior, right? Ever since her dad died, though, she had lingering guilt for not saying, "I'm sorry." She felt that he didn't know how sorry she really was because she'd never said the words.

She couldn't let that happen again.

Sitting in Eddie and Suzanne's spare bedroom, Molly talked on the phone with Liam. He hadn't wanted her to call so he could tell her how terrible she was or how he hated her. He only wanted to make sure that she was okay. He'd visited King's again and had started to worry.

Molly told him everything. She told him about the letters, about her outburst at LuLu's, about how Bennie found their dad, about Luis, Shirlington, Bennie getting drunk, losing the money, punching the bartender, Eddie and Suzanne, the King and Queen seat, and the waterfall. She felt like she was catching up with an old friend, but there was *so* much to catch up on.

Liam let Molly ramble. He always had so much patience. When she was finally done, he was silent.

"Hello?"

"I'm here. Just listening. Does anyone else know about this?"

"No. Jacey and Sam think I'm planning my dad's funeral."

"Why haven't you told anyone?"

"Because it's none of their business," Molly snapped.

"But you felt comfortable enough to tell me?"

"I mean, yeah, I guess," Molly bit the inside of her cheek hard.

"So, now you're in the bedroom of a stranger's house?" Liam laughed.

"They aren't strangers! Well, they are, but they're not."

"I get it."

"Anyway, that isn't why I called you."

"Okay, then, what's the reason?"

Molly's heart felt it was going to burst through her chest. She licked her lips, then bit her cheek again.

"I'm not saying this because I'm begging for you back or because I want us to rekindle or anything."

"Cut the shit, Moll. What is it?"

She liked when he was assertive, but it also made her cringe. He was kind, soft, and patient—everything Molly wasn't.

Molly took a deep breath, then exhaled. "I owe you an apology."

Silence.

"Hello?"

"Yeah, I'm here."

"Oh. Okay. Well, yeah, I'm sorry. I mean, I am really, genuinely sorry. What I did to you was shitty, and you never deserved any of it. You were good to me... You were *great* to me, and I fucked it up. You had every right to leave."

Silence.

"Hello?"

"Still here."

"Can you say something? Anything? Tell me to fuck off if you want to. I would."

Liam laughed again. "I'm not going to tell you to fuck off."

"Then say *something*."

"Why?"

"Because it's really quiet and—"

"No, not that. Why did you do it?"

Molly's heart dropped to the pit of her stomach. She wasn't prepared to relive the memory.

"I don't know," she said quietly.

"Did I do something to you?"

"No! Not at all!" Molly tilted her head to the ceiling, closed her eyes tight and sighed. "I just suck. And I'm sorry. I'm really, really sorry."

"I forgive you."

Molly sat silent, stunned, staring blankly at the ceiling.

"We just aren't compatible. There isn't anything wrong with that."

God damn him and his logical thinking.

"I feel bad that you uprooted your life for me, which ruined your relationship with your dad, and now…"

"It's not your fault."

"Well, either way, I'm sorry, too."

Silence.

"I think it's your turn to say something."

Molly could hear the smile in Liam's voice, and she smiled, too. "Thank you. For forgiving me and for your apology—even though it's not necessary. It means a lot."

"So, where are you headed tomorrow?"

"I have no idea. I'll find out in the morning."

"Well, wherever it is, be safe and try not to punch anyone else, will ya?" Liam laughed.

"I'll try my best."

"Same old Molly. I'll talk to you later. Goodnight."

"Night."

Molly reached over to the lamp on the nightstand and shut it off. Her phone pinged, and she saw a text from Bennie.

These walls are paper thin. I'm proud of you.

Molly laughed and rolled her eyes. Normally, she would have been embarrassed knowing her sister had heard that conversation. Instead, she was calm. She felt full.

All because she said two simple words.

When she woke up the following day, she walked down to the kitchen to Suzanne sitting at the table, reading a newspaper and drinking coffee.

"Good morning!" Suzanne said.

"Morning," Molly said, rubbing her eyes.

"Coffee?"

"Please."

Suzanne made Molly a cup of coffee, and Molly joined her at the table.

"Where's Eddie?"

"Oh, he's outside with Bennie taking care of the chickens!"

Good. Molly was happy Bennie was doing something other than moping.

"Could I use your shower?" Molly asked.

"Of course!"

Molly followed Suzanne upstairs. Suzanne handed Molly two towels and pointed to the small bathroom at the end of the hall.

"All yours!" Suzanne said.

Molly thanked her and got in the shower. The warm water felt amazing. She got out feeling refreshed physically and mentally. She felt like she had washed a ton of weight that she had been carrying for so long, right down the shower drain. She wiped the steam from the bathroom mirror with the edge of her towel, grabbed her toothbrush and toothpaste and felt every bristle against her gums.

After getting ready, she returned to the kitchen, where Eddie, Suzanne and Bennie sat, drinking coffee.

"Morning!" Bennie chirped.

"Hey, how are you feeling?"

"I'm better."

Molly gave Bennie a suspicious look. "You seem chipper."

"I feel great." Bennie threw a we'll-talk-about-it-later look. "Eddie showed me the chickens! I helped him give them food and water, **and then we** went egg hunting.

"It was a productive morning!"

"Oh! That sounds fun."

"It was!" Eddie chimed in. "She learned a lot."

"Thank you for letting us stay the night. We really appreciate it. Bennie, why don't you get a shower?"

"Already did, Mom," Bennie said, sipping her coffee and rolling her eyes.

"Oh, yeah. Okay. Great."

"I assume you girls would like this letter now, right?" Eddie asked.

They nodded.

Eddie took the envelope out of the front pocket of his yellow button-down shirt and pushed it gently across the table.

Bennie took the envelope and looked at Molly.

"Be my guest," Molly said.

Bennie opened the envelope while Molly looked over her shoulder.

Hi girls!

How has Maryland been? Have Eddie and Suzanne been treating you well? Did you get to see the King and Queen seat?

That was the spot where I proposed to your mom. It always held a special place in my heart, but for obvious reasons, I couldn't take you there.

I remember that day vividly. It was late spring, and the weather was beautiful. Flowers were starting to blossom, it was warm outside without being too hot, and everything was coming back to life.

Your mom and I were on a short weekend road trip. I had the ring in my pocket the entire weekend, but I couldn't find the perfect place. Your mom complained of being hungry, so we saw Twin Silo's on our drive, and she made me stop.

As we were walking in, we talked about where we could stop next. As luck would have it, Eddie was outside smoking a cigarette. He overheard our conversation and jumped in, making a ton of suggestions. But his most highly recommended was the King and Queen seat.

So, he drew us a map on a piece of receipt paper. I hope he gave it to you so you can follow it too. I asked him to. When your mom and I got to the spot, I decided it was the perfect time. We walked all the way out to the very tip of the cliff. Your mom stood there, her arms spread wide open, smiling towards the sky. I was behind her on one knee, waiting for her to turn around. When she did, she screamed so loud, I swear I saw birds flying out of the trees.

We went back to Twin Silo's in hope's Eddie was still there. He was. I found out later he was married to the bartender, Suzanne. I told him what happened, and he shouted, "Congratulations!" then gave me a huge hug. He, Suzanne, your mom, and I all shut down Twin Silos that night.

We spent the night at Eddie and Suzanne's house after a couple too many.

While it may seem irresponsible to trust a stranger like that, Eddie and I clicked so quickly. I had no worries about our safety.

When I came to him, and he saw me for the first time in years, he still recognized me. He still welcomed me like any time before. And when I told him why I hadn't been around in a while, he never cast judgment.

They are good people. Be sure you thank them for their hospitality.

Moving on to letter #3. If you haven't noticed by now, you've started farther away and are making your way back up toward home.   You're headed to Bethany Beach, Delaware. Your hint is: My high school girlfriend + C

Good luck!

Love,

Dad

"Do you remember her name?" Molly asked.

"Um, it was something that began with an A," Bennie said, scratching her head.

"Well, that narrows it down."

"Do you have anything better?" Bennie crossed her arms over her chest.

"Ladies!" Eddie interrupted. "What is the hint?"

"Bethany Beach, Delaware. Something to do with his high school girlfriend's name, plus the letter C," Molly said.

"Does the name Addy sound familiar?" Eddie asked, grinning.

Molly could tell he was giving them more information than he was supposed to, and he knew it.

"Addy was his tenth-grade girlfriend!" Bennie exclaimed.

"Yes! His first love. Before your mom."

"How do you know this?" Molly asked.

Eddie shrugged his shoulders. "I wasn't the only teller, you know?"

"Good memory, Eddie," Bennie said.

"It's hard to forget someone like him," Eddie looked at the floor gravely.

Molly, trying to change the subject, asked, "Okay. So, what would Addy C mean?"

"Damn it. I don't remember her last name." Bennie lightly smacked her forehead with her palm.

"I don't think it started with a C."

"Maybe you girls are reading too deep into it. Maybe C stands for something else!" Suzanne suggested.

"C... C..." Molly rubbed her temples and closed her eyes.

"C..." Bennie repeated.

Molly perked up. "What if it's not supposed to be the *letter* C? What if it means to 'see' something?"

"Or the sea!" Eddie chimed, raising a pointer finger in the air.

"Delaware has beaches. It could very well be a sea," Suzanne said.

"Addy see? Addy sea? I've never heard of Addy Sea," Molly said.

"Hold on!" Eddie yelled, slamming his hands on the table. "Addy Sea! That's the Victorian Bed and

Breakfast in Bethany Beach. Suzanne and I have been there, remember hon'?" He nudged Suzanne lightly in the ribs.

"I do! We spent a few nights! It was beautiful." She tapped Eddie on the shoulder playfully.

Molly turned to Bennie.

"Should we google it?"

"It's your stupid rule, you tell me."

Molly tried to hide a smile. Bennie was really starting to come out of her shell.

They finished up their coffee and started to pack up their things. When they got to the door, they said their goodbyes.

"Thank you for everything," Molly said, hugging Eddie.

Eddie put his hands on her shoulders. "You look just like him, ya' know that?" His eyes filled with tears.

It broke her heart when older men cried, so Molly tried to make light. "Thank god, right?" She forced a fake laugh.

"And she," he said, pointing at Bennie. "Looks just like her."

Eddie handed her a piece of paper with the house phone number.

"We have cell phones, but we aren't too good at using them!" he chuckled. "Old people problems. Please give us a call whenever."

Molly took the piece of paper and tucked it into her back pocket. The girls grabbed their bags, said one last goodbye with more hugs, and headed out the door.

Bennie drove. They had hardly made it out of the driveway when Molly finally asked what she had been wondering since last night.

"What happened?"

"With what?" Bennie tried her hardest to be vague.

"Um, well, let's talk about Tyler first."

"I told him it was over, and he could forget about the house," Bennie said flatly, staring straight ahead at the road.

"Did he respond?"

"Yeah. He said, 'Bennie, it's not what it looks like.'"

"Did you answer?"

"Nope."

"You never said anything?"

"No. I'd made my point."

"You've just been texting Luis?"

"Yep."

"How are you feeling?"

Bennie slammed on the brakes and veered to the shoulder, sending Molly into the passenger side window.

"Jesus Christ, Bennie!"

"You wanna know how I'm feeling? I'll tell you." Bennie's eyes were wide and bewildered. "I'm feeling like someone who just found their dad dead less than a week ago, and now I'm on the trip of a lifetime. I'm feeling like I deserve this experience like I deserve to be free. I'm feeling for the first time like I am living the life I *deserve*.

"I've always played on the safe side. I haven't ever broken a rule, or gotten in trouble, or done anything noteworthy. And now I'm feeling like this is my chance!" Bennie threw her arms up in the air.

Molly stared wide-eyed at Bennie.

"I'm feeling that when it comes to that idiot, I have had more fun in the last few days than I've had in the last year with him. I don't owe him an argument, or a heartbreak, or any of my tears. I'll be damned if I give him the satisfaction of seeing me heartbroken over an *accountant*.

"Dad would have had a fit!" Bennie's chest heaved. Molly could see the tiny vein across her forehead protrude. "I am feeling like someone who doesn't want to talk about it anymore and wants to just continue on this trip. *That* is how I'm feeling."

Molly couldn't hold back the wide grin on her face any longer. This was an entirely new side of Bennie that she hadn't seen before.

"Any more questions?"

Molly shook her head.

"Great." Bennie continued back on the road.

After driving for a few more miles, Molly turned and looked at Bennie.

"I'm proud of you."

Bennie gave a sideways smile. "Thank you."

"Now, about Luis."

Bennie put her palm up to Molly's face. "I've said enough. Just let it be."

"Fair."

Bennie looked at Molly through her peripheral.

"What about Liam?"

"I've said enough."

"Fair."

CHAPTER FOURTEEN

"C'mon, please tell me about Luis," Molly begged. They had been chatting while driving, and Molly was dying to know.

"There's nothing to tell you! He is a nice guy, and we've been texting. That's it."

"So, you find out you got cheated on and immediately start texting a guy you met three days ago?"

"Yes. This trip is about connecting with people and new experiences, right? Tyler tried to ruin that. Now, Tyler isn't a problem anymore."

She had a point. Still, Molly couldn't help but feel Bennie was doing this with at least a little bit of spite.

"What have you guys talked about?"

"We've talked about a lot of different things. I've mainly talked about Dad. We've been able to relate since he lost his mom, too, and that was the only parent he had. He just... gets it."

"I get that."

"What about you and Liam? How did that go?"

"You heard the whole conversation. Isn't that enough?" Molly threw her head back against the seat.

"Not the whole conversation. Just your side of it."

"It went well. Actually, it went way better than I expected it to. He's a good guy."

"So, any chance of you guys getting back together?"

"No, I don't think so. We both agreed we just weren't right for each other. But it feels good to know he doesn't hate me, at least."

"I understand. Do you want to tell me what happened?"

A small voice inside of Molly screamed, *Yes! Yes, I want to tell you everything!* Still, she hesitated.

"You don't have to."

"Maybe later."

"Whenever you're ready."

If only dad could've been here to see this. His two girls, with wildly different personalities, talking about relationships, having heart-to-hearts, and laughing together.

That's when it hit Molly. He knew exactly what he was doing when he wrote those letters.

Well done, Dad. Well done.

Molly could tell they were close to a beach when they came to their exit. She unrolled her window and smelled the salty air. Big, beautiful beach homes lined the shore. One home stood out to Molly the most. It was a three-level with two upper decks and a rounded side with big windows. She saw a spiral staircase enclosed by the rounded part of the house. She closed her eyes and imagined herself living there, gracefully descending the winding stairs in the morning in a long, satin robe, out to the deck to smell the ocean air and sip coffee.

The car slowed and pulled into the parking lot of the Addy Sea. The bed and breakfast sat perfectly on the beach. It was an older building with a historical charm of brown cedar shingles and a large wrap-around porch. Green bushes donning pink and yellow flowers were planted by the main entrance, giving it a warm, welcoming feeling.

The girls walked up the pathway to the porch. The lobby was furnished with Victorian décor. An oriental rug covered the majority of the hardwood floor, and a velvet red sofa and seat faced each other across a small marble table. A vase of flowers sat in the center, and a giant chandelier hung from the ceiling made of tin-press and painted white.

To the left was another room with a desk and two seats. Behind the desk sat a thin woman with long, curly grey hair. She smiled and waved.

"Hello! Can I help you?"

"Hi! My name is Bennie, and this is my sister, Molly. It's kind of a crazy story, but we believe our dad may have left a letter here for us. Does that sound familiar at all?"

Molly was impressed. When Bennie had first spoken to Eddie, she almost passed out.

"I believe it does. Give me just a moment, please."

The woman walked away from the desk while Molly and Bennie waited patiently. A few minutes later, she returned with an older man wearing a red suit and white slacks.

"Michael's girls!" he yelled cheerfully with an unmistakable Southern accent. He pulled the girls in for a hug and gave their cheeks air kisses.

"How are you? So sorry for your loss." He talked to them like he'd known them his whole life.

"We're hanging in there," Molly said. "It's been a hell of an adventure so far."

"I believe it! Leave it to Michael to set something like this up. Just genius. Oh! You two don't even know me! My name is Leroy. You can just call me Roy, though. And this…" he put his arms in the air and looked up. "Is my Addy Sea. Pleasure to have you. Who is who?"

"I'm Molly, and this is Bennie."

"Molly and Bennie. Great names. You have luggage, I assume?"

"Oh, are we staying here tonight?" Bennie asked.

"What kind of question is that? Yes, you're staying here, silly girl."

"Okay, thank you. I'll go grab the bags." She came back in with both of their bags, handing Molly hers.

"Aht-aht! Jason!" Roy called out to a young guy dressed in khakis and a blue collared shirt. "Take these for the girls, please?"

Jason nodded and took the bags from Bennie.

"He'll show you where your room is. Y'all get showered up and dress nice. We have a wedding tonight."

"A wedding?" Molly asked.

"Yep! It's summertime and wedding season. Lots of people want to get married at the Addy Sea. I mean, why wouldn't you? This place is perfect. Weddings here are my favorite. This red suit is my Addy Sea wedding suit."

"Who's wedding is it?" Bennie asked.

"A couple that's staying here. But never mind the details! We have two hours until martini-time and three until the wedding starts. Meet me out back on the porch at three o'clock."

Roy waved to the girls and walked away, saying hello and chatting with other guests like they were longtime friends.

Jason led the girls to the second floor. When they got to the room, he handed Molly a card with a series of numbers on it.

"This is your room code." He smiled.

"Thank you." Molly typed the code into the cipher lock and opened the door.

Inside the room were two queen beds with white comforters and red stitching. The walls had gold Victorian print, and a ceiling fan sent a nice breeze through the room. Two windows on the far wall led to a view of the beach.

Molly walked over to the window and watched as the ocean waves crashed on the shoreline, then ebbed and crashed again. A seagull swooped toward the ocean's surface and scooped something from the water. Below, she saw staff members setting up decorations and chairs for the wedding.

"I don't think I brought wedding attire," Molly said.

"I have a few sundresses if you want to borrow one?" Bennie set her bag on one of the beds and pulled three dresses out. One was black with spaghetti straps and white daisies, one was a light pink strapless dress, and one was a tan dress with thick straps.

"Can I wear the black one?"

Bennie nodded and tossed the dress to Molly. They relaxed in the room briefly before getting ready for the wedding. Molly laid back on the bed, her head sinking into the pillow as she watched the blur of the spinning ceiling fan.

"Do you ever want to get married?" Molly asked Bennie.

Bennie peaked around the bathroom door, where she was curling her hair. "Yeah, one day. Do you?"

"Maybe. I don't know."

The girls finished getting ready, and it was time to meet Roy on the back porch. He sat on a white rocking chair, sipping a martini and looking at the beach. On a small table next to him were two more martinis. Molly and Bennie joined him, sitting on the additional rocking chairs. Roy raised his glass.

"To Michael!"

"To Dad," the girls responded.

They clinked their glasses together, and each took a sip. Molly watched Bennie, excited to see her reaction to a martini. Surprisingly, Bennie gulped it down without so much as wincing.

"How did you know our dad, Roy?" Bennie asked.

Roy laughed. "You're going to find out soon!"

Bennie cocked her head but didn't ask any more questions. Instead, she looked out towards the beach. Molly looked out as well. A long path on the sand led out to the shoreline. She listened to the waves crashing, inhaling the ocean air deep into her lungs. Down the path, in the distance, she could see the wedding altar the staff had finished, covered in white and pink flowers. The view was beautiful. Molly felt like she had seen it somewhere before.

"Yeah, I sure do love it here. Lots of history," Roy said quietly, his eyes tracing the shore. "It was built in 1901 by John Addy. He was a plumber, so it was the first place in the area with indoor plumbing and gas lights, which was a big deal back then."

Roy sipped his martini.

"Come with me. I want to show you something," he said, standing up from his chair.

Molly and Bennie, still holding their martinis, followed Roy to the front of the Addy Sea.

"You see that house?" Roy pointed to a house directly across the street.

The girls nodded.

"My mother, Frances, convinced her parents to buy that house solely because some friends of hers had a house down here in Bethany Beach. Shortly after that, my father decided he didn't quite like the idea of sharing a house with his in-laws." Roy laughed. "So, he bought that house." He pointed to a house to the left.

Molly and Bennie laughed.

"Wait, wait! It gets better! Then *my* dad's parents bought *that* house!" Roy pointed to the next house.

Molly, Bennie and Roy all roared in laughter.

"I spent a lot of time down here growing up. In the beginning of the depression, they used the Addy Sea as a room and board. Bed and Breakfast's weren't quite a thing back then."

"Wow," Molly said. Something about Roy and the way he spoke was captivating. He was charming and lively.

"My family and the Addy family were neighbors. We didn't talk much, but we were cordial through the years. I got older and started working in real estate. So, in seventy-four, when they approached me about buying the property, I couldn't say no," Roy said, shrugging. "The wife wasn't too keen on the idea. Actually, she was pretty bent out of shape about it. But I had big visions for this place. I couldn't let it go."

Molly silently agreed with him.

"Bethany Beach wasn't always a tourist town. When the Addy Sea was first built, there weren't even bridges that led over this way, so most people went to Virginia Beach instead."

"We were in Virginia!" Molly said.

Roy turned and looked at them, his eyes lighting up.

"Were you!? Which part?"

"Our dad sent us to Shirlington. That was actually our first stop," Bennie said.

"And you came back!?" Roy laughed. "I never understood why anyone would ever want to leave Virginia. It's where I grew up! I raised three kids there. Two boys and a girl. They're all grown now, though. Even named my daughter Virginia—we call her Ginny for short. Anyway, my whole family is from Arlington, less than ten minutes from Shirlington."

"Small world!" Bennie chimed.

"Sure is. I went to Virginia Tech and became a civil engineer. Been bleeding orange and maroon ever since." He winked.

Roy took another sip of his martini and motioned for the girls to follow him to the back of the porch again. People in long dresses and suits started walking up the path toward the beach.

"It's almost showtime!" He grinned, rubbing his hands. "C'mon, let's go."

They finished their drinks and joined the crowd. Molly followed the crowd to find a seat, but Roy gently grabbed her shoulder, pulling her back. He shook his head.

"We stand back here," he whispered.

Molly did as Roy said. She had a feeling most people didn't question him, and she didn't want to be the first.

Finally, the string quartet started to play, and the murmur of the guests hushed. The wedding party made their way down the aisle. The girls wore gold dresses, the guy's black tuxedos with gold bowties. Everyone waited in anticipation for the bride. She finally walked down, a blonde with a curly updo and a strapless wedding dress with lace at the bottom. She looked like a princess.

The three watched as the bride and groom exchanged their vows, then sealed them with a kiss. The crowd cheered. Roy dabbed his eyes with a handkerchief, then clapped for the bride and groom. *He must know them well.*

Soon after the ceremony was over, the reception began. People congregated together on the beach, drinking, talking and laughing. Roy looked at the girls and grinned.

"This is when the real fun starts!"

He entered the crowd, Molly and Bennie following close behind. He gave hugs to the ladies and strong, firm handshakes to the men. He introduced Molly and Bennie to a few people and toasted his drink with others. He danced a little with pretty women.

Forty-five minutes had passed before a man in a purple suit started chatting with Roy and asked the question that Molly and Bennie had been wondering the entire time.

"How do you know the bride and groom?"

Roy laughed, gently tapping the man's chest.

"I'm just the landscaper at the Addy Sea!" he said, pointing his thumb behind his shoulder towards the bed and breakfast.

Molly's jaw dropped. Bennie covered her mouth and gasped.

"W-what?" the guy asked, furrowing his eyebrows.

"Yeah! I've been working all day, saw there was a wedding here, and figured I'd join." He turned to Molly and Bennie, linked arms with each of them, and walked back towards the Addy Sea.

"And that, ladies, is how I met your father."

A few hours later, and a few more martinis, Roy, Molly and Bennie sat on the porch. A candle was lit for some outdoor light, and the smell of citronella filled the air.

"I can't believe our parents got married here," Molly said. "I knew it looked familiar! Like I had seen it in pictures or something."

"I can't believe how Roy met our dad!" Bennie laughed.

"It's a true story! You saw it today; how long it takes before someone asks *if* they even ask!"

When they left the reception on the beach, Roy took them back to the porch and told them the story of how he'd met their father. The day their parents were married, he wore his red suit and white slacks, stood at the back of the wedding ceremony, and watched Molly and Bennie's parents marry.

Once the reception took place, two hours passed before their dad walked up to him and asked how he knew their mom. Roy was surprised by their dad's reaction when he told him he was the landscaper.

"Michael didn't believe me. He called my bluff right away!" Roy laughed. "Not many people do that!"

I knew it.

"He said to me, 'If you're the landscaper, then I'm the ring bearer.' I still tried to convince him, but he wasn't buying it. To this day, he's still the only one that I couldn't get one by."

Roy's eyes lowered.

"I'll miss him. He was a good man."

Molly's eyes watered a little. Hearing people tell stories about her dad and seeing how many people's lives he'd brought light to was overwhelming. Over the last few years, she had painted her dad as a villain. She'd forgotten who he really was.

"You took us there to show us how you met our dad," Bennie said. "That was so kind of you."

"Well, yes, that. And I couldn't show up without a date! I was just lucky enough to get two this time!"

The girls laughed. After a few more minutes of chatting, Roy finally slapped both of his knees and stood up.

"Ladies, it's been a pleasure, but it's far past my time to call it a night. I'll meet you on the beach first thing in the morning. Eight-thirty."

Molly cringed.

"How are we going to find you?" Bennie asked.

"I'm the only one on the beach with an orange and maroon umbrella. Remember what I said about Virginia Tech? You can't miss me."

They said their goodnights and parted ways. The girls returned to the room and got ready for bed, changing into their pajamas and taking their make-up off. Molly opened a window, and a cool ocean breeze came blasting through. She climbed into bed and drifted off, the sound of the waves helping her fall asleep.

CHAPTER 15

"Do you, Molly, take Liam to be your lawfully wedded husband?" the pastor asked.

"I do." Molly smiled at Liam, losing herself in his eyes.

"And do you, Liam, take Molly to be your lawfully wedded wife?"

"I do," Liam melted. He squeezed her hands tight with his.

"You may kiss your bride."

As Liam's lips were inches from hers, his face started to melt away. It drooped onto her shoe and all over her dress, like wax. Molly looked down, horrified.

The crowd gasped.

When she looked up, a new face formed in Liam's place. *Jake.*

Errr. Errr. Errr. Errr.

Molly sprung out of bed to the sound of Bennie's phone alarm and grabbed her chest, panting. Bennie was already awake, staring eagerly at her phone screen, smiling. She jumped when Molly woke up so abruptly.

"Jesus. You okay?"

"Yeah," Molly panted. "Bad dream."

"About what?"

"Nothing. What are you smiling at?"

"Just talking to Luis. He said he's really happy we're having such a great time."

"Oh! That's sweet."

"He's really nice. We've been having great conversations."

"I'm glad!" Molly said, getting up out of bed.

They had thirty minutes before they had to meet Roy on the beach. She hadn't packed a swimsuit, but she put on a pair of shorts and a tank top, deciding that would suffice should she decide she wanted to go in the water.

They found Roy beneath an orange and maroon umbrella like he had promised. It was easy to spot. He had two folding chairs ready for the girls.

"Morning, Roy!" Bennie called out, waving.

"Morning!" Roy waved back.

The girls sat in the chairs, and Molly dug her feet into the sand. She loved the softness of sand between her toes.

"How are you?" Molly asked him.

Roy chuckled. "Better than I deserve!"

Molly looked around the beach. It was still early, so there weren't too many people. She enjoyed the calmness, which was unlike her.

"How did you both sleep?"

"Pretty good!" Molly lied. That dream had really messed her up.

"Good!" Roy looked Molly up and down. "Are you going to go swimming?"

Molly noticed something about Roy. When he asked a question, he already knew the answer and gave you a look like you better know it, too.

The right answer to this question was, "Yes, I'm going swimming," but she didn't want to go just yet. She was still waking up and trying to shake off that dream. Before she could answer, Bennie chimed in.

"Absolutely!"

Bennie jumped up and reached her hand out to Molly. Molly sighed, dropping her shoulders in defeat. Between Bennie and Roy, Molly didn't stand a chance. She reluctantly took Bennie's hand.

Bennie nearly skipped to the water, going in up to her thighs. She laughed, bending over and cupping the water in her hands, throwing it above her head, little droplets hitting the water. Molly stood on the shoreline watching.

"C'mon, Moll! You coming in?"

"I am in!"

"Your toes are barely getting wet!"

Molly loved seeing Bennie carefree. She knew Bennie had experienced way more trauma than her regarding their dad's passing. She couldn't imagine having to find their dad—

Before finishing the thought, she blinked and saw Bennie charging at her, tackling her to the sand. She felt two small hands grab her ankles and two large ones grab her wrists. She looked up to see Roy laughing manically. She looked to her left and saw she was approaching the crashing waves.

"This was a setup!" Molly screeched.

"This is for throwing me in the stream in Shirlington!" Bennie yelled, laughing.

Roy and Bennie ran with Molly until they could barely keep her above water. They swung her back and forth as she squirmed.

"One...Two...Three!"

They released Molly into mid-air, her arms and legs flailing. She smacked the water, and a wave engulfed her body. The water was warmer than she thought it would be. She came up to the surface and gasped for air, rubbing her eyes to ease the sting of the salt water. She saw Roy and Bennie high-five.

"That was good!" Molly called out, treading water. "How did you get him involved?"

"She told me about what happened in Shirlington last night!" Roy called back. "So, we came up with a plan!"

Molly stayed in the water for a while, letting the waves take her wherever they wanted. Bennie joined her shortly after. Roy returned to his chair, enjoying the beach before more people started rolling in. Once the beach started getting busier, the girls got out of the water, where Roy was waiting with towels. They dried off and sat back down in the beach chairs.

"Well, ladies, I assume you didn't come to Bethany just to crash a wedding and play on the beach, did you?"

"No, no, we did not." Molly smirked, knowing where he was headed with this. Funny enough, she had once again almost forgotten about the letter.

Roy reached into his beach bag, pulled out a white envelope, and handed it to Molly.

"The deal is, you still need to explore a little before you go. Bethany has a lot to offer."

Molly nodded. "Deal."

Roy looked around the beach, noticing more vacationers piling in and setting up their own umbrellas. He stood up and folded his chair.

"Help me clean this stuff up, would you please? We'll take it back to the Addy Sea."

Molly and Bennie helped Roy get the beach stuff together and headed back to the bed and breakfast. The girls showered the salt water off, changed, packed up their bags, and met Roy at the same spot on the back porch. He had a plate of snickerdoodles in front of him.

He lowered his voice. "I don't do this, ever. I'm only going to offer this once, and don't ever tell anyone." He reluctantly held out the plate of cookies. "Would you like a snickerdoodle?"

"Are you sure?" Molly asked.

"No. But I like you girls. Hurry up, before I change my mind!" Roy turned his face away and shook the plate.

Molly reached over and took a cookie. It was soft, and the taste of cinnamon melted on her tongue. It was the best snickerdoodle she had ever had.

Roy peaked at Bennie, shaking the plate again.

"Oh, no thank you. I'm not a big snickerdoodle fan," she admitted.

Roy laughed. "That's only because you've never had *Sarah's* snickerdoodles. She's our pastry chef. But suit yourself." He shrugged and bit into another cookie.

"Okay, I'll try one." She chewed it slowly. Her face lit up.

"Wow, these really are good!" Bennie said, mouth half full, biting into it again.

Roy nodded, pleased that he had introduced Bennie to Sarah's snickerdoodles.

"I told ya! But they're me and Sarah's secret, so that's all you're getting." He was completely serious. "Alright, ladies. We're going to take a walk over to the Bethany Town Center." Roy stood up and clapped his hands. "But first, let me get Jason to get these bags to the car for you."

When they got to Bennie's car, Jason gently placed the bags into the trunk and shut it.

"Thanks, buddy!" Roy said.

"No problem," Jason smiled and walked back inside the Addy Sea.

"We could drive there if you want, Roy," Molly said.

"No, no! It's beautiful out. We'll walk."

Molly shrugged, and the three began walking. At every block, someone recognized and said hello to Roy. He would say hello back, and anytime someone asked how he was doing, he would respond with the same thing.

"Better than I deserve!"

They arrived at Bethany Town Center, the road lined with restaurants, stores, and entertainment. They reached an entryway with "Bethany Town Square" in bold lettering. Through the gateway were three levels of shops.

On the ground floor, they visited a candy store, Three Blonde Bakers, that sold homemade fudge with a "buy two pounds get one free" deal. Molly chose Rocky Road, Tiger's Eye, and Vanilla Sea Salt. Bennie chose vanilla, chocolate and toffee covered.

They went up to the second floor to a beach and clothing store. Molly bought a few more shirts, shorts and a bathing suit. Bennie bought a new pair of sunglasses and a baseball cap with "Bethany Beach" on it.

The third floor brought them to an arcade. Molly and Bennie, like children, went in and purchased a twenty-five-dollar game card. They played Mario Kart, Skeeball and battled each other on the Dance Dance Revolution machine—a game they used to play as kids. Roy watched them in complete joy.

After they had their fun and started their walk back to the Addy Sea, Roy leading the way, he stopped and turned to the girls.

"Your father loved you. You know that, right?" Roy's voice cracked.

"We do," Bennie answered.

"Watching you two the last day or so—the way you laughed and bantered with each other, the way you spoke about your father, the love that you have for each other and the way you've worked together and for each other during a time of grief. It's just admirable. It's something I want to make sure my kids can do one day." Roy's eyes watered. "I want to leave behind a hell of a legacy."

Bennie gave Roy a big hug. "I have no doubt in my mind you will. You've already impacted our lives so much, and we were strangers to you!"

253

"Thank you, sweetheart." Roy wiped his face and sniffled. "But I've never known a stranger."

Molly chuckled. She liked Roy a lot. He was a no-nonsense kind of guy, but he had a way of seeing the better things in life and always managed to make a joke or smile. He made his own fun, even if others questioned it sometimes, and he made his own rules. He reminded her a little bit of herself.

They made their way back to the Addy Sea and said their goodbyes. Roy air-kissed their cheeks again and gave them individual hugs this time.

"Thank you so much for having us, Roy," Bennie said.

"It was my pleasure. You girls have been a lot of fun. But before you go, can I stay to read the next letter with you?"

"Of course!"

Molly opened the trunk, opened her bag, pulled out the next letter from their dad, and handed it to Bennie. Bennie opened it and read it out loud.

Hi girls!

Isn't Bethany Beach beautiful!? It's a little brighter with Roy around for sure. Did he tell you how we met? I'm sure he did. It's one of his favorite stories.

Your mom and I were married here. It was a beautiful June day. It rained a little bit in the morning, and your mom was so worried that we would be rained out. I kept assuring her it would be fine, and it was. It finally stopped raining about two hours before the ceremony. The sand was a little wet, but other than that, it was perfect. We were married under a gorgeous sunset. It couldn't have worked out better than it did.

I hope you got to enjoy the beach as much as we did. The Addy Sea had the "home away from home" feeling that your mom and I both loved. And getting to meet Roy and his contagious personality was an added bonus.

So, now off to your next destination!

You're headed to Tuckahoe, New Jersey. It's a small town, and I mean it's a really small town, so this hint likely won't take you too long to find.

Cheesecake.

Love,

Dad

All three of them looked at each other.

"I've never heard of Tuckahoe," Molly said.

"Honestly, neither have I," Roy replied.

Bennie shrugged. "I guess we'll find out."

They said some more goodbyes and gave more hugs. Bennie hopped into the driver's seat, typing Tuckahoe, New Jersey, into the GPS. Molly glanced over to see how long it would take them. Two hours and forty-one minutes would get them there by two-forty-five.

Bennie plugged her phone into the auxiliary this time and played a song. Molly heard the beginning and smiled.

I was totin' my pack along the dusty Winnemucca Road.

When along came a semi with a high an' canvas-covered

load.

If you're goin' to Winnemucca, Mac, with me you can

ride.

And so, I climbed into the cab, and then I settled down

inside.

He asked me if I'd seen a road with so much dust and

sand.

And I said, "Listen, I've traveled every road in this here

land."

I've been everywhere, man.

I've been everywhere, man.

Crossed the deserts bare, man.

I've breathed the mountain air, man.

Of travel I've had my share, man.

I've been everywhere.

CHAPTER SIXTEEN

"This has been amazing," Bennie said as she drove.

"Yeah, it really has."

"I had no idea how many lives dad touched. Did you?"

Molly looked at Bennie blankly. "No, I didn't."

"What's wrong?"

The grief came in waves. One moment she would be lost and happy in her and her sister's travels; the next, she would be hit with a pang of sadness.

"I just miss him."

"I know, Moll. Me, too." Bennie rubbed Molly's back softly.

Molly's dream popped into her head, and she looked at Bennie.

"I cheated."

"What?" She stopped rubbing Molly's back but kept her hand there.

"On Liam. I cheated."

"Oh." Bennie covered her mouth with her hand. "*Oh.*"

"I know, I'm an asshole. I'm a horrible person. I ruin everything." Molly choked.

Bennie pulled the car over to the side of the road.

"No, you aren't," she spoke gently.

"Yes, I am! You even said it. I take things too far. I always take things too far. I didn't talk to you or dad for two years over a guy I fucked everything up with! And now I don't have the guy or my dad!" Molly started to sob.

Bennie threw her arms around Bennie and squeezed as hard as she could.

"Stop talking like that," Bennie scolded softly.

"It's not even like I want to be with Liam. I'm just mad that I— I just suck!"

"Look at me." Bennie tilted Molly's face up. "You don't suck. You're just a little... impulsive sometimes. But you don't suck. Tell me what happened."

The floodgates opened, and Molly left out no detail. She told her about how she had gotten bored with Liam. She told her about his friend Jake, who she had drunkenly slept with while Liam was dog-sitting at his parents. She told her how awful she'd felt about it the next day and how she'd immediately told Liam. She told her how he'd calmly and quietly packed his things. She told her the entire town found out the next day, and all her friends shunned her—except Jacey.

Bennie nodded and listened as Molly spoke. When Molly was finished, Bennie wiped her face for her again.

"Why didn't you want to tell me?"

"I guess I was embarrassed."

Bennie clicked her tongue. "Please don't ever be embarrassed for making a mistake. The important part is you made your amends. I heard them myself." She tucked a piece of hair behind Molly's ear in a motherly fashion.

"I'm just a shitshow," Molly sighed.

Bennie cackled. "You think you're a shitshow? Look at me! My boyfriend has been sleeping with his ex for God knows how long while I ate up every sweet thing he's said to me. I don't have enough money to buy the house, so I have no idea what I'm going to do with that. Oh, and you haven't asked me about work or how I got time off!"

"You're right; I don't know why I didn't think to ask. But you aren't a shitshow, you're responsible, you have a great job doing…"

"You have no idea what I do for work."

"Not a clue."

Bennie threw her head back and laughed. "Well, I *did* work in accounts payable. I got fired."

"What!? When!?"

"That's the real kicker. Two weeks before dad died, they let me go. I wasn't too worried because Tyler promised I could be a stay-at-home wife one day. So, yeah. I am a shitshow."

Molly lowered her head, but Bennie gently lifted her chin with her fingers.

"Listen to me. No matter how put together someone else may seem or how much better their life may look, we are *all* fucked up in our own way. Okay?"

Molly nodded.

"Now, get excited! I told Luis where we're headed next. He asked me to take lots of pictures."

Molly could tell Bennie was enjoying her conversations with Luis more than if she had just been texting a regular friend. Bennie put the car in drive and headed back on the road to New Jersey.

The girls ended up on a two-lane highway called Route Fifty-Five. They drove for a while until they saw the exit for Tuckahoe. They drove down Forty-Nine, and Molly looked around. It was a long, one-lane, straight road lined by woods and trees. They passed a boarding school, a few houses, a small gas station, a graveyard, and a library. It was secluded, just like back home. Molly felt like she belonged.

Eventually, the girls came to a bridge. The GPS announced they had officially reached Tuckahoe but nowhere around suggested they sold cheesecakes.

"What do I do?" Bennie asked.

"Just keep going straight."

They reached another light but needed to turn.

"Now what?" Bennie asked.

"Right."

Molly was guessing. She had no idea if this was the right way, but going left didn't look promising, and going right had more civilization.

Everything around the town looked historic. There was a church, a bank, and a small building with a sign that read "The Junction." Bennie pulled into The Junction's parking lot.

It was a small store made of tan cement. A black and white sign hung on the door. "Come In, We Are Open." It was filled with shelves of snacks, bread, and convenience store goods. There was a commercial refrigerator with glass doors filled with different drinks. Molly opened one of the doors, reaching for a Sunny-D. She looked over at the counter, where Bennie talked to an old, grumpy-looking man with glasses.

"Cheesecake? Do you know where I can find cheesecake around here?" Bennie yelled.

He grunted. "Make a right outta' here. Left-hand side."

"Thanks," Bennie said, defeated.

Molly put her drink up on the counter, and he manually typed the price of the Sunny-D into the register.

"Two dollars."

Molly went into her wallet and put two dollars on the counter.

"Wouldn't kill you to smile, ya' know," she snipped before walking out of the store.

The old man grunted again.

Molly got back into the car, and Bennie took off in the direction he'd given her. Despite his rudeness, he was right. Just like he'd said, on the left-hand side was a tall, old white building with a blue sign on long white posts. "Tuckahoe Cheesecakes."

The rocks of the parking lot crackled as they came to a stop. They walked up the steps to the front porch, where two people ate cheesecake at a table. They opened the door, and a gust of wind sent the smell of pastries to meet them.

The storefront was small, but Molly could see the kitchen and a stairway on the side that led to the upstairs. The glass display counter presented a few different cheesecakes. A chalkboard hung on the wall behind it with all of the flavors.

Molly looked over and saw a map. A small sign under it read, "Where, oh where, have our cheesecakes gone?" Thousands of different colored pins were marked on the map. *How have I never heard of this place before?*

A young girl with dark, curly black hair and glasses emerged from the kitchen.

"Hi there, how can I help you?"

Molly gave her the rundown, and the girl looked confused.

"I'm really sorry; I don't know who you'd need to speak with."

"Is there anywhere *else* that sells cheesecakes around here?" She'd given up trying to hide her annoyance.

"Um, no, not that I know of."

Molly took a deep breath. This girl looked as if Molly had kicked her puppy.

A heavier-set woman, who looked in her forties, came out of the kitchen, wiping her hands on her apron. She also had black curly hair, and Molly could immediately tell she was the girl's mother.

"Hi? Is there a problem I can maybe help with?" the woman asked.

Molly explained who they were and why they were there, but the woman stopped her.

"Yes! Oh, my goodness, yes. Oh no, that means he's passed." The woman frowned. This confirmed she was the younger girl's mom. They had the same thin lips and the same frown.

"Yes, he unfortunately has," Molly said.

"I am so sorry. Please, come on back."

The woman opened the small swinging door so the girls could pass through and led them to the kitchen. A few employees prepped pastries and cakes.

"I'm Ruth. I'm a good friend of your father's. That was my daughter, Sienna. I'm sorry. She's only sixteen. She doesn't know anything about your dad or what's going on."

"That's okay. I didn't mean to be rude."

It was kind of nice to not have a stranger bombard her with a hug this time. Ruth was much more stoic than the others.

"Your dad was an amazing man," Ruth said, smiling. "But I'm sure everyone's told you that already, right?"

"He was, and they have," Bennie replied.

"Well, the first thing we need to do is get you both a slice of cheesecake. I know Tuckahoe may not seem like much, but we have a lot of little hidden secrets around here."

She led the girls to a few cakes lined up on a stainless-steel table. There was regular cheesecake, chocolate chip, raspberry, and peanut butter. Molly asked for a chocolate chip, and Bennie got a slice of peanut butter. Ruth cut their cheesecakes, put each slice on a small separate plate, and led them to the porch.

The two people sitting outside when the girls first arrived were gone. Ruth, Bennie and Molly took their place at the table. Molly's cheesecake was smooth and rich. It had a slight crunch from the crust on the bottom but wasn't too crunchy. Ruth was right. This was definitely a hidden secret.

From the porch, Molly could see The Junction and the old, grumpy man standing out front, smoking a cigarette. She realized she hadn't had a smoke since Maryland.

"What's that guy's deal?" Molly asked.

Ruth squinted, then laughed.

"Who? Joe? He's not so bad once you understand him a little bit better. He actually used to be one of the happiest people I knew!"

"What happened?"

Ruth frowned the same, thin-lipped frown. "Ten years ago, his wife passed away from breast cancer. They used to run The Junction together. Some people say that when she left, a part of him left with her."

Molly's heart sank. Here she was, judging this old man and making snide remarks to him when the two of them weren't much different from each other.

They were both grieving.

They were both a little fucked up.

"He just needs a little time and patience. If you really want to win him over, take him a slice of raspberry cheesecake. He can't resist it."

"How did you know our dad?" Bennie asked. This had become the million-dollar question.

"Jeez, your dad and I go way back! He was on his way home from a trip in Ocean City, and instead of taking the parkway, he decided to take Fifty-Five."

"He drove through Tuckahoe, saw this place, and decided to stop by. He ordered a slice of chocolate chip cheesecake." She stopped and glanced at Molly, smirking. "And a water bottle."

"He asked me what else was around here, and I told him about the Tuckahoe bridge and how people like to jump from it. He demanded someone show him this bridge. So, we closed shop and showed him the way. When we got there, your dad bet us twenty dollars that he would do a backflip off the bridge. We didn't believe him. He got up on the bridge's ledge, smiled real big, and backflipped right into the river."

"No way," Molly said, taking another bite of her cheesecake.

Ruth raised her right hand. "Swear to god."

"Can we still see the bridge?"

"Sure. But right now is low-tide, and it's going to be getting dark before we know it. Sienna can take you up to the bridge tomorrow. As long as you're okay with her tagging along."

"Yeah, of course." Molly felt terrible about how she'd spoken to Sienna and wanted to make it up to her.

"Great, sounds like a plan," Ruth said. She looked at the watch on her wrist. "I'm closing up here in about thirty minutes. You're more than welcome to stay at my house. I only have two bedrooms, but I can fix the couches up really nice for you, I promise."

"We don't mind at all," Molly said, trying to reassure her.

"Perfect. I can make us a nice, homemade dinner, too."

"Do you need some help cleaning up?" Bennie asked.

"If you wouldn't mind, that would be great!"

The three got up, went back inside and started cleaning. Sienna came back and lightly instructed Molly and Bennie on what to do—how to load the dishwasher, how to wrap the cakes, and so on. They all returned to the front porch when they were done, and Ruth locked up behind them.

"You can just follow me there," Ruth said.

They followed Ruth to her home, which was only a three-minute drive. When they pulled up, Bennie parked the car on the side of the narrow street out front.

The house was a small, one-level with tan siding and a green roof. The girls followed Ruth up the cement steps and through the front door, which led into the living room.

Two tan suede couches faced each other, and a television on a small entertainment stand in front of them. The living room led to the kitchen, which was a little bigger with a sliding glass door that led to an enclosed porch. Down the hall were two bedrooms and a bathroom.

Ruth went into her bedroom and came out with two sheets, two comforters, and two pillows. She laid everything out nicely on the couches for them.

"I'm sorry; I know it's not much," Ruth said, fluffing a pillow.

"This is perfect. Don't apologize at all," Bennie reassured her.

Molly looked around the living room. There were some pictures of Ruth and Sienna in little picture frames on the entertainment stand. In one, they were standing outside of Tuckahoe Cheesecake, laughing. In another, they were on the beach. Ruth was much younger in that picture, probably in her early twenties, and Sienna was maybe two or three.

There were no pictures of a dad, though.

Ruth finished setting up the couches and turned to face Molly and Bennie.

"I was thinking I could make ribs, green beans and mashed potatoes tonight for dinner. Does that sound good to you?"

Molly's mouth watered. "Yes, thank you so much."

Ruth started cooking, and Molly and Bennie joined her in the kitchen.

"Is your husband going to join us for dinner, Ruth?" Bennie asked.

Molly shot her a glare. Ruth put the ribs in the oven and turned around.

"I-I'm sorry. I didn't mean to be rude; I just thought..."

"That's okay. Don't worry. Unfortunately, no. He actually passed away four years ago. Car accident." Ruth scrunched her nose.

"O-oh. I'm so sorry."

"No, no! It's okay, really."

"Can you tell us about him?" Molly asked.

Ruth beamed. "His name was Dave. He was a great guy. We started dating our freshman year of high school. He was really the one who made the bet with your dad about doing a backflip.

"I adored him. We were inseparable from the very beginning." She sighed. "We really did everything together. He saw this house for sale when we were only nineteen and promised me he was going to buy it for us.

"No one believed we would make it because of how young we were. And I get it. But Dave wouldn't take no for an answer, and he bought this house. He stayed true to his word."

She took a deep breath.

"I was working one day when the sheriff came by and told me about the accident. He was headed home from work, and someone ran a redlight."

Ruth looked around the kitchen.

"I could afford more—Tuckahoe Cheesecake does well—but I feel like I'd be selling his legacy. I know it probably sounds stupid."

"Not at all," Molly said.

"It hasn't been easy. I'm the only person Sienna has now. She and her dad had such a close bond. She's so sweet, but she's shy. She gets picked on by other kids her age, and I can only do so much about it. I put her in therapy which has seemed to help a bit."

Molly's heart ached for Sienna. She wanted to march into her room and hug her.

"Anyway, I didn't want to say anything about it, given your recent circumstances. We manage and make do. But can I give you girls a little bit of wisdom?"

Molly and Bennie nodded.

"Figure out what makes you happy and forget what anyone has to say about it. Go pursue whatever you want to pursue. Because the only thing that's promised out of this story we make for ourselves is that it comes to an end."

Goosebumps trickled down Molly's arms.

Once dinner was done, Ruth called Sienna to come eat. The four of them sat at the high-top kitchen table and dug in.

The food was delicious. Molly hadn't had a real home-cooked dinner in a long time, and she'd forgotten how much better it was than eating out.

Once they finished dinner, they all helped clear the table and put the dishes away. Ruth went into Sienna's room and pulled out some board games. She had Sorry, Life, Monopoly, and Yahtzee in her hands.

"Do you girls like games?"

Molly nodded.

She set the games down on the table. The first one she picked was Yahtzee.

"This is me and Sienna's favorite thing to do, right?" She grinned at Sienna.

Sienna smiled back and nodded.

They played a few board games, laughing and chatting with each other before it started to get late. They cleaned up the games, and all made their separate ways to end the night.

The couch was comfier than Molly expected it to be. Her mind started to wander. Luis had lost his mom. Grumpy Joe from The Junction had lost his wife. Ruth had lost her husband. Sienna had lost her dad. They had lost their dad.

All of them had different ways of handling the grief. Luis told lots of stories about his mom and spoke highly of her. Joe was still grieving ten years later. Sienna didn't really talk at all. Ruth didn't have any pictures of her Dave anywhere in the house, but despite being able to afford somewhere bigger, she stayed in this little home he'd worked so hard for.

And Molly and Bennie were out chasing letters.

She found it intriguing that all of them had experienced something so similar but dealt with it in such different ways.

CHAPTER SEVENTEEN

The following day, Molly woke up before anyone else—with no alarms or assistance—and walked downstairs to the back porch.

She watched two birds flutter around each other and into the trees. She listened to them singing. A lovely summer breeze came through the porch screens, and she took a deep breath.

"Good morning," she heard a quiet voice say.

She turned and saw Sienna standing at the sliding glass door.

"Hey, good morning," Molly said.

"My mom went to work, but she said you guys wanted to see the railroad bridge." Sienna beamed.

"Yeah, for sure!"

"Well, I know it's early, but it's high tide right now. Probably the best time to go."

"I guess we should go wake up Bennie then?"

Sienna grinned and nodded. "Make sure you put bathing suits on."

"I don't think I'm going to jump."

Sienna shrugged. "Even if you don't, you can still swim."

"How far away is it?"

"I ride my bike there. It takes ten minutes, tops. I have two extra bikes, too. One is my old bike, and one is my mom's. You guys can ride those."

They went inside and woke Bennie. Each girl took a turn in the tiny bathroom to get ready. Sienna led them to the shed in the backyard and pulled out three bikes. They were the cruiser bikes—the kind you see on boardwalks—with big wide handlebars. They each jumped on their bike, and Sienna led the way.

As they peddled, Molly saw the river on the left. They passed a house built on pile-dwellings, sitting directly on the river. She could see the railroad bridge but couldn't see how they were going to be able to get to it.

The girls came up on a cul-de-sac, and Sienna stopped, got off her bike and put the kickstand down. Molly and Bennie did the same. There was a slight opening in the trees that they could walk through. Sienna went first, pushing some branches out of the way.

The railroad bridge was old, the tracks made of what was now rusted metal and wood. To the right, Molly saw a train station with old industrial trains, and to the left was the bridge.

"Do trains actually come through here?" Molly asked.

"Sometimes, but they're really slow."

The three walked down the tracks. Molly watched her feet, the rocks crackling underneath her.

They made it to the bridge and could see the water through the track's gaps.

Molly jumped up onto the bridge's thick, flat guardrail. She looked out, watching the morning sun continue to rise. On the right of the river were tall, thin reeds, and on the left was the house that sat on the water. She wondered what it would be like to live there.

Sienna hopped up with her, eyeing the water.

"Are you going to jump?" Sienna asked.

Molly looked down. It was about a twenty-foot drop. She shuttered.

"I don't think so."

"Suit yourself!" Sienna plunged into the water, feet first.

Molly and Bennie gawked. This little sixteen-year-old girl had just thrown herself off a bridge. They looked down at the water, waiting for Sienna to surface.

Molly held her breath for a few seconds. When Sienna's head popped up from the water, she exhaled.

"C'mon!" Sienna yelled. "It's not so bad!"

Molly looked at Bennie.

"Not a chance," Bennie said.

In the distance, they heard engines rev. They looked down towards the train station and saw three people on quads riding down the train tracks, headed their way.

Now, *that* was more Molly's style. She and Liam used to ride quads all the time.

Sienna swam to the riverbank and climbed back to the bridge. The three on quads stopped and took off their helmets. They were young boys around Sienna's age.

Molly looked over at Sienna, whose face had gone pale.

"Look who's here!" one of the boys said.

"Hey, Sienna," another one said softly.

"Hi," she said quietly, looking at the ground.

"Out here bridge jumping alone again?" another one teased. Molly could tell he was the ringleader.

"Please, just leave me alone."

"Aww, Sienna, it's okay to be a quiet weirdo. I would be too if my dad was dead," Ringleader said, tapping Sienna on the cheek.

The boy that had softly greeted Sienna smacked Ringleader in the chest.

"Too far."

Ringleader rolled his eyes.

"What's the problem?" Molly butted in.

"Who are you?" Ringleader spat.

"Doesn't matter. She said leave her alone. So, leave her alone."

Ringleader looked back at his friends and laughed.

"Or what?"

Molly thought for a minute. This was a sixteen-year-old kid. She certainly couldn't punch him, or she'd end up in jail, but she could stoop to their level. She looked at the quad.

"You like to race?"

The boys laughed.

"Yeah, we do," Ringleader said.

"Okay, cool. I'll take your slowest quad, which from the looks of it..." She pointed to one of the boys standing behind Ringleader. "Is yours. And I'll race all three of you, one by one. For each of you that I beat, you have to kiss Sienna's feet and tell her how sorry you are. And then you stop fucking with her from that point on."

"Okay. So, what if you lose?" Ringleader asked, smirking.

"If I lose…" She thought for a moment. "I have to do a backflip off of the bridge."

She couldn't believe she'd said that, but she still put her hand out, and all three boys shook it.

The kid with the slow quad hopped off, and Molly took his seat. She started the quad and pointed to Ringleader.

"You first!" she yelled over the purring engine.

Ringleader smiled, jumped on his quad, put his helmet on, and started it up.

They both turned to face the train station.

"There and back!" Molly yelled.

Ringleader nodded.

The nice boy stood between them and put both hands up.

"Three…two…one." He threw his hands down, and they took off down the tracks.

Grab the clutch, let go of the gas, kick the shifter, grab the gas, second gear.

The engine roared, indicating she had to shift.

Grab the clutch, let go of the gas, kick the shifter, grab the gas, third gear.

It roared again.

Ringleader was ahead of her, but not by much.

Grab the clutch, let go of the gas, kick the shifter, grab the gas, fourth gear.

She started gaining on him.

Grab the clutch, let go of the gas, kick the shifter, grab the gas, fifth gear.

The wind flew through her hair. She squinted, the force of the wind causing her eyes to water.

She was neck and neck with Ringleader. Noticing they were approaching where they had to turn around, she watched Ringleader down shift.

Grab the clutch, let go of the gas, kick the shifter, grab the gas, sixth gear.

She zoomed ahead of him, spun around in sixth gear, and headed back to the group at the bridge.

She looked behind her, but all she could see was a cloud of dust and a slight shadow of Ringleader.

She rode past the nice boy, waiting with his hands up. He swooped them down as she passed. Sienna and Bennie cheered.

A minute later, Ringleader rode up, stopped, and turned his quad off.

"How the hell can you ride like that?"

"I've had some practice."

She raced the next kid and did the same thing. *First gear, second, third, fourth, fifth, sixth, and keep it there until you can't anymore.*

She beat him, too.

While racing the nice kid, she'd started off strong like she had with the other two, but on the way back, her tire clipped the edge of one of the railroad tracks, and she had to downshift into third. Nice boy flew past her, winning the race.

Shit.

She rode back up to the group and turned the quad off, defeated. She looked at the three boys.

"Well, a deal is a deal," Molly said.

Both boys looked at Sienna, who stood smugly, her arms on her hips. She pointed to her sneakers and looked at the two boys who'd lost up and down. They rolled their eyes, then got on the ground and kissed Sienna's feet.

"We're sorry, Sienna," they mumbled.

"I can't hear you," Sienna mocked, cupping her ear with her hand.

"We're *sorry,* Sienna," they said louder.

"And?" Molly prodded.

"And what!?" ringleader yelled.

"And you're gonna leave her alone from now on."

"And we're gonna leave you alone from now on," the boys said in unison. They got up and looked at Molly.

"Deals a deal. Liam beat you."

Molly froze. *Of course, his name is Liam.* She took a deep breath and looked back at the railroad bridge, then at Bennie, who shook her head.

"You're right," Molly said.

She stripped down to her bathing suit, hoisted herself onto the bridge's guardrail, and stood with her back to the water. Her heart throbbed, and her knees weakened as she looked down at the water. She hadn't done a backflip off of anything in five years, and now she was about to do one off of a twenty-foot bridge.

She looked at Bennie. "Record this."

Bennie took her phone out and started recording.

Sienna ran up to Molly, grabbing her arm. "You don't have to do this if you don't want to. Those guys suck, anyway."

"Yes, I do." Molly lightly pulled away from Sienna. She took another deep breath, looked at Bennie, the three boys, and Sienna, smiled, and back-flipped perfectly into the water.

The last thing she heard before she hit the water was Bennie screaming.

"Holy shit!"

The water was deep. Way too deep for Molly to even get close to the bottom. The bubbles tickled her body as she floated back up to the surface. All three boys, Bennie and Sienna looked down at her.

"That was awesome!" Liam yelled.

"Your turn, Bennie!" Molly called up.

She was surprised to watch her sister strip down to her bathing suit and hop on the guardrail. Bennie held her hand out, and Sienna took it.

"Holy shit, she's really gonna do it," Molly muttered.

On cue, Bennie and Sienna jumped—Bennie screaming the entire way down. The force of them hitting the water sent a splash toward the sky. When their heads popped up, Bennie gasped for air.

"That was terrifying," she said breathily.

Molly laughed. "Do you want to do it again?"

"Absolutely not."

The girls swam out of the river, climbed the hill, and threw their clothes back on.

"Can I see the video?" she asked Bennie.

Bennie nodded and opened her phone, showing her the video.

"Holy shit," Molly whispered.

The boys started their quads to leave, but mini-Liam walked up to Sienna before they did.

"Hey, just so you know, I've always thought Ryan was an asshole."

"Thanks," Sienna said shyly, turning to cover her face a bit.

Mini-Liam smiled and hopped on his quad. The boys headed in one direction, and the girls headed in another. As they rode back, Sienna turned to look at them.

"My mom said to go to Tuckahoe Cheesecake after the bridge. We can stop at my house first so you guys can get your things, though."

"Okay!" Molly said.

They continued pedaling until they'd gotten back to Ruth's house. They put the bikes back in the shed and went inside. Molly and Bennie changed out of their bathing suits and into dry clothes, then packed their bags. The three girls piled into Bennie's car and headed to Tuckahoe Cheesecake.

Ruth was at the counter, counting cash.

"Hi! How was it?"

"It was amazing!" Sienna announced before the girls could say anything.

Ruth laughed. "Wow! You're excited today. I know you love it. What about you girls?"

"It was a great time," Molly said, trying to spare the details.

"Mom, Molly did a backflip off of the bridge!"

Molly bit the inside of her cheek, waiting for Sienna to tell Ruth about the racing and the boys. She didn't.

"There's a video."

"Let me see it!"

Bennie pulled out her phone and showed Ruth the video. Ruth looked up slowly at Molly.

"You are your father's daughter," she said, smiling and shaking her head. "Sienna, can you go to the kitchen and help Riley with some cheesecakes?"

Sienna nodded. She ran to Molly and Bennie, giving each of them a hug.

"Thank you," she whispered to Molly.

Molly nodded and smiled.

Sienna went to the kitchen, and Ruth returned the cash to the register.

"I guess it's time for your letter," Ruth said. "Give me one second."

She walked to the kitchen and returned with an envelope in her hand. *Letter #5.* She handed it to Molly.

Tuckahoe has a lot more to it than you'd think, doesn't it?

Molly laughed. Even from the other side—if there was another side—he had proved her wrong.

I met Ruth and Dave while I was coming back from meeting friends in Ocean City, New Jersey, but the parkway was bumper to bumper. So, I decided to take some back roads. I saw Tuckahoe Cheesecake and had to stop in for myself.

When it comes to small towns, I've always been intrigued by what the people around the town did for fun. So, I asked them what there was to do around Tuckahoe. When they told me about the bridge, I decided I had to see it.

I'll tell you a secret. When we got to that railroad bridge and I saw how high up it was, I was terrified. I hadn't done a backflip off a diving board, let alone a damn bridge. But I wanted to show off. And luckily, I was successful.

The part Ruth probably didn't tell you about was that Dave felt he had been shown up a little. So, he followed suit, back-flipping off the bridge right after me. He smacked the hell out of his back and knocked the wind out of himself. But he never showed it, and I never said a word about it, even though I could tell. Guys are stupid like that. He admitted it a few years later.

Every summer after that I would go down to Ocean City, and on my way home I would stop by Tuckahoe Cheesecake to see Ruth and Dave. And I had a slice of chocolate chip cheesecake every time I stopped. I never did jump the bridge again, but I sure did visit, watching sunsets.

Dave's passing hit me hard. What hit me harder was not attending his funeral. Please tell Ruth that I'm sorry. I couldn't bring myself to do it when I saw her last.

I hope you girls saw the bridge. More importantly, I hope you jumped too. For me and for Dave.

Well, you only have two letters left after this one. I hope I've made it as special as I can so far. This next place you're going is one of my absolute favorite places. You're headed to Cortlandt, New York.

Your hints are:

1. Cue balls in Peekskill
2. Anthony Hogan's nose

Love,

Dad.

Molly looked at Bennie. "I have no idea what that means. I don't even know who Anthony Hogan is."

"Can you look it up?" Ruth asked.

"No, because Molly made up this stupid rule."

"Why not just start driving to Cortlandt? You might see some more clues when you get there."

"Dad said there are seven letters. We're coming toward the end of this trip anyway. We might as well go there, drive around, and try to find something. Worst thing that happens is we get to see new places," Molly said.

"Sure! Yeah!" Bennie said sarcastically, throwing her arms up in the air. "Let's just go to the town we've never been to, and I'm sure it'll just come to us out of thin air!"

"That's kind of what happened in Maryland!" Molly reminded her.

Bennie sighed, rubbing her temples. "Fine. Whatever."

The girls said goodbye to Ruth and Sienna and got into the car.

"Wait!" Molly yelled.

"What!?"

"I forgot something."

Molly got out of the car and ran back inside.

"Ruth!" she called out.

Ruth came out from the kitchen.

"Can I get a slice of raspberry cheesecake, please?"

"Sure, of course." Ruth opened the glass display and pulled out a slice of raspberry cheesecake.

"How much?"

"Now, you know damn well I'm not going to charge you for that."

Molly smiled sheepishly. "Thank you."

"Of course. Be safe!" Ruth said, waving to Molly as Molly headed out the door.

Molly got back in the car. "Can you stop back at The Junction, please?"

"Why?"

"Can you just do it? Please?"

Bennie drove over to The Junction and parked.

"I'll be right back," Molly said.

She walked inside and saw Joe stocking canned vegetables.

"Excuse me," she said.

Joe turned and looked at her. "Yeah?"

Molly handed the box to Joe.

"Ruth told me this is your favorite. I'm sorry for being rude to you the other day."

Joe's scowl softened. He slowly took the box from Molly with shaky hands.

"Thank you. Thank you very much. This was my wife's favorite." He smiled.

"You're welcome. Have a great day, Joe."

Molly turned and walked out of the store, getting back into the car.

"All good?" Bennie asked.

"Yeah," Molly said, looking through the glass door of The Junction.

She watched as Joe walked over to the counter and opened the box. He grabbed a plastic fork from behind the counter, gently put it in the cheesecake, then took a bite. He smiled and looked up. She watched and read his lips as he looked up and said, "thank you,".

"All good."

CHAPTER EIGHTEEN

Back through the wooded roads and up forty-nine, the girls listened to music with the windows down, enjoying the warm summer afternoon.

"What was the cheesecake for?" Bennie asked.

"I gave it to Joe."

"Who?"

"The guy at The Junction. Remember, Ruth told us about him?"

"Oh, yeah. I forgot about that. Why?"

Molly looked over at Bennie.

"I was kind of rude to him the first time. I wanted to apologize."

Bennie raised her eyebrows. "You apologized?"

"Yes," Molly said proudly. "I did."

"I don't believe it."

"I did!"

"So? How did you feel? Did it hurt?"

Molly pushed Bennie's shoulder playfully. "No, it didn't hurt. It actually felt good."

Bennie's phone pinged. Molly glanced down and saw Luis's name on the screen.

"How's that going?" Molly asked.

"It's going," Bennie said, shrugging her shoulders. She grabbed her phone and sent a text back. "So, I might be planning a trip back to Shirlington after this."

"Oh yeah?"

"Luis and I have been talking about it. I'd like to see him again. But he did joke that we can't ever go back to Patty's."

Molly laughed. "Even if we could've gone back after the first night, we definitely can't now."

She looked out of the window, watching the trees flash past her. She stuck her hand out, the warm wind dancing through the gaps of her fingers. She closed her eyes and felt the sunshine warm her face.

She wished her dad could have seen what she'd done for Joe. He would have been so proud of her for saying those silly, simple words.

I'm sorry.

Her eyes quickly opened again when she heard the sound of a blaring car horn. They were crossing into opposing traffic and about to be in a head-on collision.

"Shit!" Bennie screamed, quickly veering the steering wheel to the right.

She veered too hard, sending them toward a telephone pole on the grassy side of the road. Molly's head smacked against the passenger door. Her ears rang from the impact, and her vision blurred.

Bennie veered again, clipping the telephone pole with the side view mirror, wiping it off the car. There was a loud pop, and Molly turned around to see rubber debris flying behind them.

"You blew out! Hit the brakes!"

"What do you think I'm doing!?"

"Hit them harder!"

Bennie lifted her right leg and slammed her foot on the brakes with as much pressure as possible. After a few seconds, the car finally came to a screeching stop.

Both girls sat in the car on the side of the road, gasping.

"Are you okay?" Bennie asked.

"Yeah, I think so. Are you?"

Bennie nodded. Her hands still gripping the steering wheel, shaking.

"Just stay here," Molly said, getting out of the car to look at the damage.

Bennie's back passenger tire had completely blown out and was now nothing but a ruined rim. She squatted down, pushing her hair back with her fingertips.

"How bad is it?"

Molly saw Bennie standing over her, picking at her nails.

"I said stay in the car, Bennie."

"I need to know how bad it is."

"Pretty fucking bad!" Molly yelled.

Bennie stepped back.

"Where is your spare?"

"I don't have one," Bennie whispered.

"What?"

"I don't have one!" Bennie said louder.

"How?"

"Tyler needed—"

"Just stop. Don't. Don't even finish that sentence," Molly said, holding up a hand. "How?"

Everything had happened so quickly; she wasn't even sure how Bennie had managed to end up on the other side of the road.

"I was answering Luis," Bennie said quietly, picking at her nails forcefully.

"Oh my god."

"I'm sorry, Molly. I didn't mean to! I just—"

"You just what? You just weren't paying attention? Texting a guy who you've known for less than a week was more fucking important than getting to our next destination in one piece? You just didn't think about that?" Molly shrieked.

Bennie whimpered softly.

"Oh, for Christ's sake, spare me the tears, Bennie. I'm getting sick of seeing them from you. You do realize I have a life back at home that I need to get to, right?"

Molly was fuming, losing all mindfulness or filter.

"I don't live in this fairytale world where two sisters travel all over without a care. I have shit that I have to take care of! And I don't even know who to call about this!" She motioned towards the car.

"I said I was sorry! It was an accident!"

"How could you be so stupid!?"

Bennie took a step towards Molly, scowling. She wasn't sad anymore; she was pissed.

"You wouldn't even be here if it wasn't for me, you know that, right?"

"Yeah, I would say so!"

"You know what I mean."

"I don't! Why don't you tell me?" Molly demanded, throwing her arms up in the air.

Bennie took another step towards Molly, close enough that Molly could feel her breath. Bennie poked Molly's chest hard.

"If I hadn't found that letter or been nice enough to tell you, you wouldn't be on this trip. If it weren't for *my* car because yours is a complete piece of shit, we wouldn't have been able to go."

"Back up, Bennie."

"No." Bennie poked Molly again, harder this time. "The irony is incredible, honestly. You are the first person to pass judgment when someone else fucks up or when they do something that inconveniences you, yet you ruin *everything* you touch."

"I don't."

"You do!" Bennie let out a sarcastic laugh. "You had a great relationship. You fucked that up and lost all your friends in the process. You left your *family* behind to go be with a guy you couldn't even stay loyal to and work at a shitty diner in the middle of nowhere! And look at you!" Bennie waved her arms at Molly.

"You couldn't even say you were sorry until six months later to someone you hurt. You haven't even said you're sorry to me!"

"Sorry for what?"

"For leaving me for two fucking years!" Bennie screamed.

A few moments passed in silence.

"You left. I took care of dad without even knowing he was dying. I did everything. I cleaned, I cooked, I gave him medicine, I *fucking found* him!" Bennie turned around and kicked the car, leaving a dent in the rear bumper. "And I haven't even got so much as a thanks from you! How can you be so goddamn selfish?!"

"I'm not selfish."

"Oh, no? How's your cat, Molly? How's Jacey doing back at your house? Any ideas?"

"None of your business!" Truthfully, she didn't know the answers to those questions.

"Right. You couldn't be bothered to ask."

"You know what? Fuck this trip. And fuck these letters. I'm done." Molly turned and started walking down the road.

"There Molly goes again! Ignoring her issues! I've got news for you, sweetheart! You can move as many times as you want and run away from all your problems, but you'll always be a miserable, ungrateful bitch!"

"Don't call me sweetheart!" Molly yelled without turning back.

Molly planned to call Jacey or Sam to come get her. She walked until Bennie was out of sight, then pulled out her phone.

No service.

"Great!"

The summer sun that had felt so good on her face a moment ago wasn't as pleasant anymore. Sweat poured down her forehead. She wiped it with the back of her hand. She considered turning around and going back to the car, but she shook the thought from her head. She wasn't going back to Bennie.

An occasional car would pass, and Molly would hope someone would stop and offer help, but each car left her in a gust of hot wind.

Occasionally she'd check her phone, hoping for a signal, but it was a dead zone. She kept walking. Sooner or later, she would find a spot with service and call Jacey. New Jersey wasn't too far of a drive from home.

Maybe Bennie was right. Maybe she was a little bit selfish, and maybe she did tend to run away from her problems. That didn't make her a bad person, though, right?

She continued walking until she came upon a little red gas station. Her throat was dry, and she needed to rehydrate, so she stopped to grab something to drink. She rechecked her phone—still no service. The gas station store probably had a phone she could borrow.

The bell chimed, and the door slammed behind her, making her jump. A tall, skinny guy in a royal blue hoodie was at the counter, buying lottery tickets from a short, dark-haired girl with thick-framed glasses.

Molly went to the drinks, opened the door, and grabbed a water bottle. She untwisted the cap and chugged half of it, then wiped her mouth with the back of her arm. She didn't care that she hadn't paid for it yet; she was parched.

The woman working and the man in the hoodie were talking in hushed voices. Molly walked up to the counter and examined the woman closer. She was young, probably around Molly's age, and her eyes were wide as she spoke with the man.

Molly looked down at the counter and realized the man was holding something.

It was a knife.

She gasped quietly, then covered her mouth with her hand. The woman glanced over at Molly; her eyes full of worry.

Molly mouthed, "Are you being robbed?"

The woman nodded quickly but subtly, then looked back at the man, still trying to reason with him.

"I don't want to hurt you. I just want money."

Molly stayed calm and quietly walked around to the back of the store. She crouched down and peaked from behind the corner of the shelf.

The man's voice grew louder.

"Just give me the money!" he yelled, jabbing with the knife.

"Okay!" The woman jumped back and started opening the drawer, taking out cash.

Molly closed her eyes and breathed as deeply as she could.

1…

2…

3.

On three, she ran as fast as she could, staying low, grabbed the man from around his waist and tackled him to the ground.

"Call 9-1-1!" Molly called out to the woman behind the counter. She cocked back and punched the man in the face with her left hand.

Selfish.

She punched him again.

How's your cat?

She punched him again.

Miserable, ungrateful bitch.

She punched him again.

The man screamed and finally threw Molly off of him. They both stood up. He still had the knife in his hand.

Shit.

The man charged at her, but she dodged him. He spun around and stared at her.

"What are you, a fucking hero?"

He charged at her again, holding the knife in the air. This time, Molly grabbed one of the shelves and threw it on the ground, blocking him. Chips and snacks soared as the man stumbled over the shelf and fell.

Molly ran for the door, but the man reached her first, grabbing her by the hair and throwing her on the ground. He stood over her, grinning wickedly. She lifted her foot up and kicked him in the groin.

He yelled in agony, clutching his stomach, and fell on top of her. Molly wiggled, trying to get out from underneath the man, but he managed to reach over and grab her throat, squeezing.

"Stupid," he snarled. He swung the knife into the air.

Molly grabbed his arm, holding it away from her with every ounce of strength she had. It was getting harder to breathe.

"Look at the hero now," he flashed a wicked, yellow grin.

"Fuck you," Molly choked, still holding his arm. Her palms were sweating, and she was starting to lose her grip. Her arm shook as she tried to keep his knife-wielding hand away.

Her hand slipped. She shut her eyes tight and turned her face, which was starting to go blue. How was her sister supposed to live with the loss of two family members? Would she see her dad again? How would Bennie get home?

Spare me the tears.

Molly gasped for air but got none.

I don't live in a fairytale world.

She grabbed the man's hand on her throat, her eyes still closed, trying to get him off her.

I'm done with this trip.

It was going to happen again. Her last words to someone she loved were going to be horrible. Her heart shattered.

Suddenly, there was a loud crack. The pressure from her throat lifted, and the man's body collapsed onto hers.

She opened her eyes, wheezing, taking in all the oxygen her lungs could handle. Her vision was blurred. She blinked hard, but nothing changed. She could only see blurry shadows around her.

Standing above her was a girl holding a wooden baseball bat and a man ripping the guy off her, throwing him to the side with all his force.

She blinked hard and rubbed her eyes.

"Bennie?"

She blinked harder.

"Joe?"

CHAPTER NINETEEN

Joe helped Molly off the ground. Bennie stood behind him, still holding the wooden baseball bat in the air.

"Oh my god, I think he's dead." Bennie dropped the bat, letting it fall to the ground.

The three looked over the man lying motionless on the floor.

"Oh my god, he's dead. I killed him! He's dead!" Bennie paced around the room, grabbing at her hair.

Molly knelt down next to the man.

"I didn't mean to! I swear I didn't mean to! Holy shit. He's fucking dead."

"Bennie," Molly said.

"He's dead, isn't he? Oh my god. I didn't even know you were here! I saw Joe and got in the truck to find you, and then we stopped here for gas."

"Bennie."

"And then I saw him! And I saw you! And then I saw a baseball bat in the corner. And my instincts kicked in, and I just— I just swung. And now he's dead!"

"Bennie!" Molly yelled.

Bennie stopped pacing and looked at Molly.

"He isn't dead."

"W-what?"

"He isn't dead. You just knocked him out." Molly pointed to the man's chest, which was moving up and down.

Bennie released an exasperated sigh and sat on the ground, holding her head in her hands.

"Holy shit. Holy *shit*," Bennie panted.

The woman working behind the counter came running out from the back.

"Are you all okay?" She looked down at the man on the floor. "Holy shit."

"We're fine," Molly said.

Sirens rang in the near distance.

"That's the police. They should be here any minute. Would you mind making a statement?" the woman asked.

"No time for that!" Joe spoke up.

Molly squinted at him. "Why?"

"You wanna make it to New York at some point or not?"

"We should make a report," Bennie said.

"You got cameras in this place?" he asked the woman.

"They've been broken for months. They're just for show at this point. Stuff like this doesn't happen around here." Her voice shook as she spoke.

"Good," Joe said, turning back to Molly.

"We have about ninety seconds until approximately seven troopers fly through this parking lot, guns loaded. You stay and make a statement, and they take you to the station. Then you'll have to go to court, which could take months. Do you want to come back here for court?" he asked, raising an eyebrow.

Molly shook her head.

"Didn't think so." Joe looked back at the woman.

"This girl here saved your life. I think the least you could do is not have gotten a good enough look at her for a description, right?"

The woman gulped, then nodded.

The sirens were getting louder. Joe helped Bennie off the floor.

"C'mon, get in the truck. Hurry up!"

Before the three could leave, the woman grabbed Molly's arm.

"I just want to say thank you so much."

Molly looked down at the woman's hand on her arm. It wasn't her voice that was shaking; it was her body.

"You're welcome, but please... I was never here."

The woman gave her a knowing look.

"Let's go!" Joe yelled out from the truck.

Molly ran over and jumped into the backseat of the old, rusty truck. Joe threw the shifter into reverse and peeled out of the parking lot.

As they drove back down forty-nine towards their car, seven troopers passed them, sirens roaring and lights flashing red and blue. Molly couldn't help but feel excited like she had just fled her own crime scene.

Sitting in the passenger seat, Bennie turned back to look at Molly.

"Are you okay?" she asked.

"Yeah, I'm okay."

Joe pulled off to where Bennie's car was parked. The three of them got out of the truck. Joe knelt and assessed the damage.

"I have so many questions," Molly said.

Bennie laughed. "You? *I* have so many questions."

"Thank you for what you did back there. It was probably the most badass thing I've ever seen you do."

Bennie's eyes sparkled. "You think so?"

"Absolutely. Quick thinking. I liked it."

Bennie did a curtsy. "Thank you."

"So, how did you end up with Joe?"

"When you didn't come back after a while, I got nervous. I walked in the direction that you went, but I couldn't find you, and I started to panic. Joe drove by and saw me frantic. Turns out he doesn't even live in Tuckahoe. He lives up forty-nine a few miles."

Molly felt satisfaction knowing Bennie had come looking for her.

"He didn't realize it was me at first. He just stopped because he saw an upset young girl on the side of the road. He asked if I was okay, so I explained what happened and that I was looking for you. I told him you were the girl who gave him the cheesecake."

"How did you end up at the gas station?"

"Joe was running low on gas. That's the only reason we stopped."

"Dammit!" Joe yelled from under the car. "Forgot to get that, too." He stood up, dusting off his pants. "Well, the good news is, by the grace of god, you somehow didn't screw anything else up besides your mirror and the tire."

Molly let out a sigh of relief.

"Bad news is, I won't be able to get you a new tire until tomorrow."

Molly groaned.

"I could not help ya' at all if ya'd rather?" Joe said, leaning up against Bennie's car. "Your choice."

"No, no. It's not that. It's just—"

There's no such thing as a coincidence in this world. What does exist is only the inevitable.

Molly getting the cheesecake for Joe and apologizing, the accident, storming away and ending up saving someone. Joe passing Bennie as she walked and ending up at the same gas station as Molly—none of it was a coincidence. If you asked Molly, it was fate.

"Okay," Molly said. "Where do we stay?"

"You can stay at my place for the night," Joe answered.

"This is how women get kidnapped." Molly crossed her arms, putting one leg out to the side.

"Lady, I am eighty-eight years old. She just took down a grown man far younger and stronger than me." Joe pointed at Bennie. "And from what this one's told me, this ain't your first time."

Molly smirked, straightening up a bit.

"If I tried to kidnap you, you'd probably have me dead in three minutes."

"Probably."

"That, and I don't want ya'. You staying or what?"

"Yeah, we'll stay."

"Okay. The auto store is closed for the day, but first thing in the mornin', I'll take ya' over there, we'll get a tire, and we'll get ya' back on the road."

"Thanks, Joe."

"Mhm."

The three hopped in the truck and drove back up the road. When they passed the gas station, the thief was being pulled out on a stretcher—sitting up, alert, and very much alive.

"Look, Bennie, he's not dead!" Molly laughed, pointing.

"Thank God. Asshole."

Joe kept driving for a few miles until he turned onto a dirt driveway.

"This is it. Ain't much, and I only have two bedrooms, so one of ya' will have to take the couch. But it's better than nothin', right?" Joe opened the truck door and jumped out.

It was a small, yellow house with chipping paint. The screen door didn't close all the way, the grass stood high, and a junk pile filled with old cars, car parts and metal filled the side yard.

"Well? You just gonna sit there, or are ya' coming inside?"

Maybe Molly could call Ruth and get a ride back to her house. Or maybe there was a hotel nearby. But how would she say that without offending Joe? He was their only shot at getting back on the road.

Unsurprisingly, the inside of the home was no better than the outside. It wasn't dirty, but it was cluttered with random stuff. Mountains of unopened mail sat on a small table next to the green sofa in the living room. The walls were bare; there were no photos or décor. Boxes were stacked messily in corners.

The kitchen walls were made of small yellow tile, and again, things were scattered across the kitchen table and counters—magazines, books, dishes, and more mail. The sink was full of dishes.

"Sorry, I wasn't expecting company." Joe started pushing the things on the table aside, clearing as much as he could so that they could sit down.

"It's okay," Bennie tried to reassure him.

As they sat down at the table, a letter with red, bold capital letters caught Molly's eye.

FORECLOSURE NOTICE

She squinted, trying to read as much as she could without Joe noticing.

Past due payments…

Mortgage…

Contract…

Two thousand dollars…

"My wife would have my neck right now if she was still here. Allowing company with the house looking like this." Joe chuckled, looking around the kitchen.

"It's fine. We just appreciate your help," Bennie said.

"Don't mention it."

"Do you have any family around?" Molly asked. She bit the inside of her cheek. Maybe she shouldn't have asked.

"I have a daughter. She doesn't live around here, though. She's all the way out in California with her husband and kids."

"Do you get to see them?"

"Can't afford to."

Molly saw right through Joe's grumpy demeanor. He was sad. Lonely.

"But she calls. Sometimes. And she sends me pictures of the grandkids. A girl and a boy. Ten and thirteen. Haven't seen em' in a few years."

"I'm sorry," Bennie murmured.

"That's okay. I make do."

"Can you tell me more about your wife?" Molly asked. She bit her cheek again.

"Depends," Joe said, crossing his arms across his chest and leaning back in his chair. "Can you tell me more about your dad?"

The girls took turns telling Joe stories about their dad and what he was like. They talked about how much fun he was and how he was always laughing. They talked about how he would light up any room he walked into. They talked about his love for travel. They told stories about growing up, how even though their mom wasn't there, their dad always made up for it. They wanted for nothing. He gave them everything a child could ask for.

When they finished, Joe smiled. "He sounds like he was quite a man."

"He was," Bennie beamed.

"What about your wife?" Molly asked.

Joe sighed. "My wife. Her name was Amelia." He stopped, leaning his elbows onto the table and folding his hands together. "She was my backbone. Truly superwoman if you ask me. She supported every dream I had, even The Junction. She left her job to help me open it. Everyone told her she was crazy, but she believed in me. Sometimes, I still wonder why."

Molly's eyes watered as Joe spoke. His tone was low and sad.

"She took care of the house while I ran the store. Sometimes she would stop by and surprise me with lunch. She ran a tight ship, that's for sure. And she had the purest heart."

He paused again, taking another deep breath.

"She was diagnosed with breast cancer. The doctors said the odds of recovery were promising with treatment. So, we went through everything. The chemo, the radiation, all of it. And at first, it did work."

Bennie put a hand on Joe's shoulder, comforting him.

"Six months later, at a follow-up, we found out it'd come back and spread." Joe's voice cracked. He sniffled, wiping one eye with his index finger. "When she passed, I was a wreck. I closed The Junction for four months. I couldn't pull myself out of bed. I couldn't eat. I couldn't even smile. All these boxes are all things of hers that I can't look at anymore."

Joe grabbed a Kleenex off the table and blew his nose.

"She passed five years ago. I'm still not over it. I don't think I ever will be."

Molly wanted to ask if Joe not opening The Junction for months was why he was at risk of his home being foreclosed, but instead, she finally kept her mouth shut.

"I've tried picking up hobbies to keep me busy. That's what the pile of junk is outside. I can't ever really stick to something, though." Joe stood up from the table and cleared his throat. "So, now I'm just trying to play catch up. Just seems that every time I get close, something else gets thrown at me that pushes me back again."

Molly knew the feeling well.

Joe looked at the clock on the kitchen wall; it was already eight-thirty.

"I'm gonna go lay down. I'll make sure you get that tire fixed, and you're on your way tomorrow. There's a bedroom down the hall here, and then there's the couch in the living room. Feel free to either of those." Joe walked down the hall to his bedroom and shut the door behind him.

"I feel so sorry for him," Bennie said.

"Me, too. Look at this." Molly picked up the foreclosure letter and handed it to Bennie.

"Really? All over two-thousand dollars?"

"Poor guy can't catch a break."

"Maybe we could do something nice for him? Clean the place up a little bit?"

"I don't know. He doesn't seem like the kind of person who's going to appreciate two strangers going through his things."

Bennie twisted her lips to the side. "I guess you're right. Let's sleep on it, maybe?"

"Yeah. You can have the bedroom."

They parted ways, and Molly laid down, covering herself with the small, knitted pink blanket that was draped over the top of the couch. She shut her eyes, but she couldn't sleep. All she could think about was what had happened earlier at the gas station, how she thought she was going to die, and about Joe.

Her phone pinged; it was Luis.

Hey! Hope you guys are okay. I haven't heard from Bennie since this morning.

Hey. Yeah, we're fine. We had a long day today. I'm sure she'll text you tomorrow.

Okay, awesome. She's a great girl.

Yeah. She really is.

He had no idea how great Bennie really was.

She tossed and turned restlessly, unable to calm the loop of events in her mind. Finally, when thinking about Joe, she sprung up from the couch with an idea.

Molly tiptoed through the house to the bedroom where Bennie was sleeping. She creaked the door open slowly, hearing Bennie lightly snoring. Her eyes adjusted to the darkness as she walked up to her sister and shook her lightly.

"Bennie. Bennie!"

"What?" Bennie whispered back, still not opening her eyes.

"How much money do we have left?"

Bennie slowly sat up. "What?" she asked again, rubbing her eyes.

"How much money do we have left?"

"Plenty, why?"

"Enough to part ways with two thousand of it?"

"I think so?"

"Then I think we just found a way to help Joe."

CHAPTER TWENTY

Both girls got up early, but Joe was already dressed and making coffee.

"You ready to get on the road?" Joe asked.

"Absolutely. Before we go, do you have a piece of paper and a pen I can borrow?"

Joe fumbled through his junk drawer for a minute before pulling out some paper and a pen and handing it to Molly.

The girls got ready for the day and headed to the truck where Joe was waiting. They got in the truck and headed to the auto parts store.

"Did you sleep okay?" Joe asked them.

"Just fine," Molly answered, sitting in the passenger's seat.

"Good."

They pulled into the parking lot of the auto parts store, and Joe looked over at Molly, then back at Bennie.

"You two stay right here. I'll be out in a few minutes."

After ten minutes, Joe came out of the store, holding up a tire and pumping it in the air victoriously.

"Let's go fix that hunk of shit!" He laughed.

Molly worried that Bennie's car wouldn't be there when they got back, that maybe someone had reported it as abandoned and had it towed. Her worries washed away when they pulled up to where the crash was, and the car was still there.

Joe parked and got out, going into the bed of his truck and rummaging through tools. He grabbed the things he needed, slid himself underneath Bennie's car, and got to work.

Molly and Bennie sat on the ground a few feet away, watching him.

"Thank you again," Molly said.

"For what?" Bennie asked, tilting her head.

"Well, you kind of saved my life yesterday."

"I did, didn't I."

"You did."

"I didn't defend you back in Shirlington. I couldn't let that happen again."

"All I could think about was dying."

"What?"

"During the whole fight. All I could think about was the last things I said to you. And the last thing's I said to Dad—" Molly's voice squeaked.

Bennie put an arm around Molly, pulling her in close, and Molly leaned her head on Bennie's shoulder.

"It's okay. I said terrible things to you, too. I didn't mean them. I'm sorry."

"You were right, though. I can run all I want, but running doesn't mean it's fixed. Running doesn't mean I'll be happier."

Joe slithered out from underneath the car and brushed himself off, sending clouds of dirt in the air. Molly waved it away and looked up to see a brand-new tire on the car.

"Good as new, sort of," Joe said. "Just gotta take care of that mirror, but that won't stop you from getting to where ya' need to be."

"Thank you so much!" Bennie cheered, jumping up and giving Joe a hug.

"You're welcome," he said, trying to hide a smile.

Bennie ran to the driver's side and jumped in, yelling out in celebration as she started the car. Molly walked over to Joe and put a hand on his shoulder.

"Thank you so much. For everything."

"Don't mention it. Glad I could help."

"I have something for you." Molly reached into the back pocket of her jeans and pulled out an envelope.

"I don't want it," Joe said firmly, turning away from Molly.

"You don't even know what it is."

"I could take a guess."

Molly sighed. "Someone recently told me a quote about how there are no such things as coincidences and how anything that happens is inevitable. It's pretty much a fancy way to say that shit happens for a reason."

Joe slowly turned back towards Molly, trying to piece together what she meant.

"I believe that everything that has happened in the last twenty-four hours was supposed to happen. We, for whatever reason, were supposed to crash the car and meet you. And you, for whatever reason, were supposed to meet us." She waved the envelope at him. "Take it."

Joe paused, then slowly took the envelope from Molly.

"Thank you," he said.

"It was nice meeting you, Joe. We appreciate your help."

"C'mon, Moll! You ready?" Bennie yelled from the car.

"Yeah, I'm coming! Take care of yourself."

She got into the passenger seat and shut the door.

"Bye, Joe! Thank you again for everything!" Bennie yelled, waving her hand out of her window.

Joe waved back.

"Hurry up, go, go, go," Molly whispered.

Bennie put the car in drive and hit the gas, sending a cloud of dirt trailing behind them.

Molly turned around as the dirt cloud cleared and watched Joe open his envelope. He pulled out the letter, and two thousand dollars fell to the ground. He looked up as the girls drove away, threw his face into his hands, and fell to his knees.

Bennie grinned, turning and looking at Molly. "What did you write?"

Molly smirked. "Just a nice letter."

Dear Joe,

You can buy all the cheesecake you'd like.

Or you can keep your home.

Love,

Your Inevitable's

As the girls drove, Molly couldn't help but feel unsettled. Neither of them knew what the clue meant. With the recent setback, they didn't have much time to mess around. She looked for signs of somewhere to play pool or something that said "Anthony."

"Who is Anthony Hogan?" Molly asked.

"I have no idea."

"Would it be against the rules to look him up? Maybe I can learn something about him to help us get where we're going."

"I think that's still fair game."

Molly pulled out her phone and typed in "Anthony Hogan." She scrolled for a few minutes, but all she could find were random people on Facebook and out-of-state businesses.

She paused, trying to figure out if there was something else she could try. She typed in a new search.

Anthony Hogan. Nose.

A few scrolls down, she found a website for a place called Anthony's Nose in Cortlandt, New York.

It was a rock formation that had gotten the name "Anthony's Nose" from its former owner, Pierre Van Cortlandt, in 1697. He named the peak after Anthony Hogan, a pre-revolutionary war sea captain. Anthony was known for the structure of his nose, and Van Cortlandt felt that the cliff resembled it.

She closed out before seeing any pictures, not wanting to ruin the view for herself.

"I think I know where we're going, but it's only the second half."

"Well, do you want to go backwards?" Bennie asked.

"Why not, right?"

"Sure. Where are we going?"

"Anthony's Nose."

"What?"

Molly put her hands up. "I swear to God, that's what the place is called. I'll put it in my GPS."

They had a little over an hour left before they'd arrive. As they briefly passed through New York City, Molly looked out at the water, the mid-morning sun's reflection shimmering off its surface.

They continued through the busy city highways, hitting traffic snags occasionally. People beeped their horns, weaving in and out where they could. Molly looked at Bennie tapping her fingers on the steering wheel.

"Are you okay?"

"I'm fine. This is just…a lot."

"Do you want me to drive?"

"No. I can do this."

And she did. Any time they reached traffic, she followed the patterns of the local city drivers—weaving in between cars, working her way through traffic until they finally made it through and could continue driving.

"Have you talked to Luis?"

Bennie shook her head, tapping her fingers on the steering wheel again.

"Why?"

"I don't know. I don't want to tell him about what happened."

"What happened?"

Bennie looked over at Molly, her eyes wide. "I almost killed a man," she said, keeping her voice low like she feared someone would hear.

Molly threw her head back and cackled. "You didn't almost kill him. You knocked him out."

"I could have killed him!"

"Either way, what does that have to do with Luis?"

"I don't want him to get the wrong impression of me."

"You vomited all over a public bar in front of him, and that was when he decided he was in love with you."

"He isn't in love with me."

"Whatever. Just don't tell him the part about you almost killing a man," Molly mocked, laughing again.

"What?"

"Yeah. Tell him we spent an extra night in New Jersey, and now we're on our way to New York."

Bennie looked at Molly like she'd shared some secret sorcery. "I guess you're right." She picked up her phone, and Molly grabbed her wrist.

"Don't you dare open that phone while you're driving. It can wait."

Bennie laughed and put her phone back into the cup holder. "Fair enough."

The busy highways started to dissipate, and the roads widened, offering more lanes with less traffic. Lines of tall trees replaced graffitied brick walls, and the straight highways turned into sharply curved roads. They crossed another bridge, Bear Mountain Bridge. Bear Mountain stood tall above them. Molly looked down at her GPS; they were only seven minutes away.

"It says it's coming up in half a mile," Molly said, uncertainty setting in.

She could only see a lake to the left, and rocks piled high to her right. Cars were parked along the road, but she didn't see an entrance or sign indicating where to start the hike.

"I guess just pull over and park. The GPS says we're here."

Bennie pulled over and parked in between two other cars. The girls got out, looking for any signs of a trailhead. They only found a steep mountain covered in large rocks and towering trees. Molly saw a small wooden booth perched a few feet above them on the hill. She climbed up to look at it, but all that was there were some old, worn newsletters hanging on a bulletin board.

She looked at the trees and saw that some had trail reflectors nailed to them. She turned and looked down at Bennie, shrugging.

"I guess this is it," Molly said, pointing to the trees.

"There's no way."

"Only one way to find out."

Bennie slowly climbed up to the information booth.

"I don't know if I'm going to be able to do this," Bennie said.

"It'll be fine! C'mon."

The girls started following the reflectors on the trees. They climbed over rocks, their legs already starting to ache. Their chests tightened as the hills inclined, and their breathing became sharp and shallow.

"Can we stop for a second?" Bennie asked, squatting down and putting a hand on her chest.

Molly nodded, sitting on the ground next to her. Her shirt was sticking to her, thanks to her sweat. She peeled it off and shook it out, trying to get some circulation.

"We can do this," Molly panted.

"I don't think I can do this."

"C'mon. It has to be close."

They stood up and continued hiking, following the reflectors until they reached another hill of rocks and trees.

"I need one more break," Bennie said, this time sitting down on one of the rocks. She wiped the sweat from her face with her palms. "I can't breathe."

Molly gave Bennie a few minutes to catch her breath before they began again. Bennie made it a few more minutes this time before she sat.

"Molly, I really don't think that I can do this." Bennie clutched her chest, breathing heavily.

"Do you want to stay down here?"

"I don't want to, but I just don't think this is for me. My legs feel like they're on fire, and I'm having a really hard time catching my breath," Bennie said in between deep inhales. Her eyes were filled with tears.

"Okay. Okay. It's alright."

"It's not alright. We are so close to being done. I want to experience everything."

"This is an experience in itself. You don't *have* to do anything."

"But Dad would—"

"Dad would be proud you even tried this. I'm going to keep going. You stay down here. I'll be back soon. Call me if you need me, alright?"

"Thank you."

Molly looked up at the remainder of the hill she had to climb. She took one deep breath and started hiking again.

Her legs burned, and her muscles ached as she trekked over giant boulders, climbing as best as she could. Her lungs felt like they could burst from her rib cage at any moment, and a sharp pang occasionally shot through her chest.

When she finally reached the top, she was happy to be met with flat ground. She leaned against a tree, placed her hand on her chest, and moaned. She saw a sign a few feet before her with an arrow pointing right.

Anthony's Nose.

"Almost there," she encouraged herself.

Her breathing and heart rate started to drop back to normal. She walked by a small lake and looked out. The sun was hitting it just the right way, so its reflection beamed off the water like someone in the sky was saying hello. She smiled.

After a few more small, far less treacherous hills, Molly found another sign pointing toward Anthony's nose. She climbed a bit further until she found the rock peak. It gave a perfect view of the mountain and Bear Mountain Bridge, which stretched across the Hudson River.

The view was incredible, but it didn't feel the same without Bennie. After a few minutes of taking everything in, Molly turned around to head back.

Passing the lake again, she looked over, hoping to see the sun's unique reflection on the water again, but it wasn't there anymore. Her phone started ringing in her pocket.

Bennie.

"Hello?" Molly answered.

"Oh my God, I see you."

Molly looked up, and there ahead of her stood Bennie, slowly but surely making her way up.

"Oh my God!" Molly hung up the phone and ran to Bennie, hugging her. "I'm so proud of you!"

"I had to do it. I would be so mad at myself if I didn't do it."

"Let's go!"

"How much farther?"

"Not far at all."

"I need one more break."

Molly laughed. "Take all the breaks you need."

Bennie only needed that one last break before they finally got to Anthony's Nose together. Molly turned to Bennie and smiled as if she were showing her a secret treasure.

This is what their dad wanted—to show them these secret treasures, to share the feelings of excitement and giddiness. Molly hoped that wherever he was, he could see everything and feel her same sense of fulfillment.

"Can we sit up here for a while?" Bennie asked.

"Sure."

Molly took in the shades of green that covered the mountains and hills, the way the river's water moved, and the way the wind was warm but still gentle and cooling. With Bennie, she felt complete.

The way back down the mountain was far easier than the way up. No breaks were needed, and when they finally reached the bottom, they looked back up, victoriously.

"We did that," Molly said, pointing up.

"Yes, we did," Bennie replied proudly. "But I don't think I'll ever do it again."

They walked back to the car, Molly driving this time.

"I guess we need to find somewhere to play pool now?" Molly looked at the last letter her dad had written them.

"I guess so."

"Do you want to just say screw the rule?"

Bennie pursed her lips. "Typical."

"What?"

"You and breaking the rules."

Molly grinned. "Well, sometimes rules are made to be broken."

"Go for it then. It was your rule anyway."

"Yes, Bennie. You've reminded me plenty of times."

Molly grabbed her phone and looked up *bars near Peekskill*. The first thing to come up was a bar called The Public.

"I guess we can start here, and if this isn't it, we just keep looking," Molly said. She typed it into her GPS—eight minutes.

As they drove off, crossing the Bear Mountain Bridge, Molly looked back briefly up at the peak they were just standing. She wondered if anyone was looking down.

They pulled up to The Public. The small front parking lot was full, so Molly parked on the side of the road. They got out and headed towards the bar, but the usual glowing neon beer signs were dim, and the inside looked dark.

"Is it open?" Bennie asked.

"I have no idea."

They walked up to the door and pulled on the handle. The door swung open, and Molly turned to Bennie.

"I guess it is."

The girls walked in and sat down at the bar. A few men sat at the other end, sipping beer from frosted glasses and chatting while watching the television above the bar. Molly could hear the loud ticks from pool balls bouncing off each other from a separate room. The bar itself was made of glass, with thousands of pennies inside. Molly admired it, wondering how it was made. Liquor bottles of all kinds sat lined on shelves behind the bar, ceiling lights putting them on display.

The girls grabbed a drink menu and waited for someone to greet them. Molly read through the drinks, looking at the cocktail options, when she heard a woman softly gasp. She glanced up from behind the menu.

A tall, thin woman with brown hair above her shoulders looked familiar to Molly.

"Hi," the woman said softly, approaching Molly slowly. Molly thought it was a strange way for a bartender to greet a guest.

"Oh, fuck no," Bennie said.

Molly turned and looked at Bennie. Bennie threw the menu down on the bar and pushed the stool out, screeching across the floor, and stormed towards the door. Molly got up to follow her.

"What? What's wrong?"

"Bennie, wait!" the woman called out, but it was too late. Bennie had already walked out.

Molly spun around to ask the woman how she knew Bennie's name. She stared for a moment before time froze around her. She could no longer hear the chatter of the men with their beers. The pool balls stopped clacking together, and the entire bar was silent.

Short, wavy brown hair. Thin, tall frame. The

eyes.

"Mom."

CHAPTER TWENTY-ONE

Molly ran to the car where Bennie sat in the driver seat, gripping the steering wheel, her knuckles turning white, staring straight ahead.

Molly grabbed the passenger side handle, but the door was locked. She knocked on the window.

"Bennie. Open the door."

Bennie didn't even look at Molly.

"Bennie! Open the door!" Molly pounded on the window, harder this time.

Bennie looked at Molly. Her eyes were not lowered in sadness, but instead, they were fierce. Piercing. Rageful. Cold.

Bennie unlocked the door, and Molly slowly got it. Bennie turned her head back towards the road and stared.

"Bennie, I—"

"I hate her."

"I get it, I do. But I—"

"No," Bennie said quietly. "You nothing. You have no idea how I feel. You don't even know her."

"You're right, I don't. But we have to get that letter."

"Fuck that letter. And fuck her."

Molly sighed. "Would it be okay if I went in and got the letter?"

"Do whatever you want," Bennie snapped.

"You aren't going to leave me here stranded if I go back inside, right?"

"No."

"I'm just going to go in, get the letter, and then we can leave. Okay?"

"Yep."

Molly got out and went back into the bar. Her stomach did flips as she reached for the door handle, but she stuck her chest out and walked in.

Their mom stood at the bar, her head in her hands, pushing the hair out of her face. Molly made a beeline for her.

"You know why we're here. Give it to me."

"Molly, please give me a chance to—"

"Stop," Molly raised a hand. "I'm not here for that. Just give me the letter."

"Meg, can I get another Miller?" one of the guys called out, drunkenly oblivious to the shitshow that was happening.

"It can wait!" Molly snapped at him.

Meg went into the register, typed in a code, and the till slid open. She reached in and pulled the envelope out, walking back to Molly and handing it to her.

"Here."

Molly snatched it out of her hand.

"Please, if I could just talk—"

"I don't even *know* you," Molly hissed. "And that woman that just walked out of that door? She is the closest thing I have ever known to a mom. You should be thanking her."

"I know. I'm not asking for forgiveness. I'm just asking for a chance to explain myself."

Molly ran her tongue across her teeth and sat down.

"You have three minutes."

"I know there's nothing I can say that will justify what I did to all three of you. I'll regret it forever."

"Two and a half."

Meg laughed. "Oh god, you are just like—" She looked away. "Never mind. I had a lot of personal issues that I had to figure out on my own, and those issues hindered me from being able to be a good mom."

"Were you doing drugs or something?"

"No, it wasn't that. I just— I didn't know how to be a mom."

"I feel like most people figure that out as they go." Molly narrowed her eyes.

Meg sighed. "I had parental depression."

"You're joking, right?"

Bennie was right. This is a waste of time.

"It's a real thing! Please, just listen."

Molly motioned with her hand for Meg to get on with it.

"Having parental depression made me everything I *didn't* want to be as a mom. I had a hard time caring about you or Bennie's needs. One of you would cry if you fell or got hurt, and it was like my head screamed to help you, but I just couldn't."

Molly didn't remember this, but she did remember that it was their dad who was there any time she or Bennie needed something.

"I didn't know at the time what I had. I thought I was a sociopath. What kind of mom doesn't swoop in to protect their child at the first sense of danger? What kind of mom can't feed her babies, or fall asleep cuddling them, or—"

"What kind of mom *abandons* her kids?" Molly hissed.

"The kind that thinks she doesn't deserve them."

"You didn't."

"You're right, and I still think I don't deserve you. I don't think I deserve you or Bennie's forgiveness. But I do think that you both deserve closure, especially Bennie."

"Excuse me," the same man who had asked Meg for a drink earlier quietly interrupted. "Could I—"

"Hang on, Frank!" Meg snapped, holding her pointer finger out at him.

The man sunk back into his seat.

"I ran. I ran because I thought it would fix me, it would fix your dad, and it would fix you girls. When I ran, I still couldn't eat, or sleep, or find joy in anything. Nothing changed, other than I didn't have my family anymore."

Molly softened. She knew the feeling of running far too well.

"It wasn't until I was at my breaking point that I got help. Your dad had begged me to do it, but I wasn't ready then. I finally got myself into therapy and on medication, which took forever to find one that was right for me. When I finally felt free again, it was too late to come back into your lives. Your dad and I discussed it. At that point, you were seven, and Bennie was ten. It wouldn't have been right to disrupt your lives like that."

Molly was quiet. She didn't know what to say, and she didn't know how she was going to tell Bennie.

"I don't forgive you," Molly said. "But I do understand."

Meg smiled softly. "That's all I can ask for."

Molly took one good look at her, knowing this would be the clearest and last memory of her mom.

"Take care of yourself," Molly said.

"You, too, honey. You, too."

Molly returned to the car, opened the door and got in.

"Do you want to hear about it?" Molly asked.

"No."

"Do you want to read the letter with me?"

"No. Just read it and tell me where we're going."

"Well, the next letter is the last one, and this trip has, without a doubt, been the shortest. Maybe we could go explore or—"

"I don't want to explore!" Bennie yelled. Her face was red. "I want to get this last letter, and then I want to go the fuck home."

"Okay."

She slowly opened the envelope.

Hi girls,

As I'm sure you now understand, there's a reason this letter was towards the end. I'm sure there are a range of emotions. Molly, you didn't know much of your mom, and Bennie, you knew enough, but not nearly the extent.

Your mom always suffered from depression, but it got worse after you girls. That is in no way blaming either of you - please don't take it lightly when I say that you both had absolutely nothing to do with this. And after many years, I was able to come to peace with the fact that I wasn't to blame either. Your mom has taken full responsibility.

It started off with her not being able to eat. Anything that I made, she wanted nothing to do with. She lost weight rapidly, and I begged her to see a doctor. She wouldn't. But she still tried her best for you girls. She would still tend to your needs, and force herself to go to school functions, Bennie's soccer games, things like that.

Then her sleep schedule started taking a turn. She would sleep all day, which made me solely responsible for getting you girls to school from school and packing lunches while tending to her as much as I could. Then she would be awake all night. I would try to comfort her and ask her to talk to me, but she wouldn't.

Then I started noticing changes in her behavior towards you both. She just seemed to stop caring. She didn't rush to your side when you needed her. She didn't have any interest in feeding you or bonding with you. She no longer came to school functions or soccer games. But it wasn't just you she'd lost interest in. She lost interest in me, her friends, her livelihood. She was a shell of a human.

I didn't know where she was going, she wouldn't tell me, but I knew she was leaving. She just said she needed to go figure things out for herself. She knew she didn't "fit in" with the town. When she missed Bennie's parent-teacher conference, I felt the judgment from other parents. When she wasn't picking Molly up from daycare, I could hear the teachers in the back asking where she was. When she missed soccer games, the moms of the other kids would tell me how much of an "involved" dad I was.

When I finally did hear from her years later, you both had grown up more and had developed your own little (big) personalities. Our marriage was undoubtedly over, but we discussed her coming back into your lives and agreed that her popping back up wouldn't be best for either of you. We had just built a solid foundation for ourselves. To introduce you to split holidays, birthdays, and weekends with essentially a stranger wouldn't have been fair.

I have never and will never condone her actions or how she went about what she did, and neither will she. But I hope you can find it in your hearts to understand. It took me some time, too. But life is too short to be angry forever. Forgiveness is not an attribute of the weak, and I believe I have raised some incredibly strong young women. That doesn't mean that your mom should now be an active part of your lives. It just means that both of you, especially Bennie, can move forward in peace.

Now to the last letter:

Go to McDermott's funeral home. I'll be there waiting, but don't worry, it's not my body, haha! Talk to Greg. You'll figure it out from there.

Love,

Dad

Greg was the funeral home director and one of their dad's very good friends. She should have known this was where he was taking them.

"Bennie, I need you to read this," Molly said, holding the letter out to Bennie.

"No."

"Now."

"I said no."

"Bennie! I'm going to tell you something a good friend of mine told me. You *know* what the right thing to do is. You are just refusing to do it, and no one else is going to have the balls to tell you that you're acting like a b—" Molly reflected on Jacey's word choice. "Brat. If you don't read this letter, you'll never forgive yourself. Just like you wouldn't have forgiven yourself if you hadn't climbed that mountain."

Bennie looked at Molly, her expression finally softening. She took the letter and read it. After she was done, she put the letter gently in her lap and looked up at the ceiling, sighing deeply.

"I wish I hadn't read that."

"Why?"

"Because now I have to go in there and do the right thing." Bennie got out of the car and walked back into The Public. Molly followed.

Bennie swung the door open and walked up to the bar. Meg's face dropped when she saw Bennie again. She slid the drinks to the men and walked over to the girls.

"Bennie—"

"I forgive you."

"What?"

"I forgive you. But I'm not forgiving you for you. I'm forgiving you for me. This doesn't mean you get to be a part of my life now. This just means I can continue on with mine."

Meg nodded, pursing her lips, her eyes filling with tears. "That is more than what I could ask for."

Bennie turned around and walked back out of the bar.

"How do you feel?" Molly asked once they were back in the car.

"I—I don't know yet."

"I don't really know her, so I don't feel as strongly about it as you do. But I am really proud of you. I know it wasn't easy."

"I feel like I can move on now. I used to wonder if it was my fault. I was so angry at her, and I just didn't realize how much it affected me."

"Are you ready to go home?"

"Yeah, I am."

"Are you sure? We came all the way out here."

"Molly, that was a lot to take in. I need to go home."

"Well, let's go then."

Molly put the address for the funeral home into the GPS—two hours and forty-five minutes. Bennie put the car in drive, and they began their last journey.

For the first hour, they drove in silence. Molly wanted to give Bennie some time to process everything.

She didn't want to risk upsetting her, but she needed

something to entertain her.

"Can we put on music?" Molly asked.

"Sure."

Molly turned the radio on, and the FM played

through the speakers.

I've been to Pittsburgh, Parkersburg, Gravelburg,

Colorado, Ellensburg, Rexburg, Vicksburg, El Dorado.

Bennie shot a look at Molly, who quickly lifted

her phone up to show Bennie it wasn't connected to the

car.

"This is the radio."

Larimore, Atmore, Haverstraw, Chatanika

Chaska, Nebraska, Alaska, Opelika.

Bennie managed to crack a smile and start

singing along.

Baraboo, Waterloo, Kalamazoo, Kansas City.

Molly joined in with Bennie, and both girls started singing as loud as their lungs would let them.

Sioux City, Cedar City, Dodge City, what a pity.

I've been everywhere, man,

I've been everywhere, man,

Crossed the desert's bare, man,

I've breathed the mountain air, man

Of travel I've had my share, man

I've been everywhere.

CHAPTER TWENTY-TWO

At about four o'clock, the girls finally pulled up to McDermott's Funeral Home. Bennie parked, and both got out, stretching their legs and arms.

"Well, this is the last letter," Molly said.

It was bittersweet. She was excited to see what the last letter had in store, but she was sad that the adventure was coming to an end.

"It is," Bennie said, pouting a bit. Molly could tell she felt the same way.

"Do you want to take a day? Come back tomorrow?"

"No. We've come this far."

The girls walked up the large, concrete steps. The building was white, with a red door and large windows. They were met in the lobby by Greg's receptionist, Leann. Leann was short and heavier, somewhere in her sixties, with long gray hair braided to the side.

"Hi, girls," Leann said softly, hugging them. "I'm so sorry about your dad. Let me go ahead and get Greg for you." Leann scurried down one of the halls.

A few minutes later, Greg came out with a beautiful navy-blue bag. He set it on the ground to give the girls a hug. They had known Greg for a long time but never really talked about what he did for a living. Molly didn't know why she hadn't thought of reaching out to him.

"How was your trip?" he asked.

"It was definitely an adventure," Molly said, smiling.

"I'll tell you what, only your dad could pull off a stunt like this," Greg said as his eyes watered. "He was an incredible guy and a great friend." He picked the bag back up and handed it to Molly. "Here's the last one. But please wait until you're in the car to read it, okay?"

"Sure."

"Good luck, girls. And if you need anything, you know where to find me."

They thanked Greg and walked out of the funeral home.

"The letter is in the bag. Should we read that first?" Molly asked.

"I think that would be the most appropriate."

Molly took the letter out, trying to divert her eyes from anything else in the bag.

Girls,

This is the last letter of your trip, but it doesn't mean the adventure is over. The adventure is never over.

You can find adventure in different places, people, or things. You can find adventure driving down the street and seeing something new being built or walking a new trail you've never visited before. You can find adventure in love. You can find adventure in the warmth of someone else's arms. You can find adventure in your family and friends. Adventure is everywhere, as long as you're looking for it.

You can even find adventure in your own backyard.

For years I've watched you girls in that backyard. I've watched you play hide and seek, tag, or whatever make-believe game you both came up with that day. I've heard your laughs, your cries, your yells for Dad, coming right from that backyard. I've watched you collect lightning bugs in jars, I've watched you and your friends play back there, and when you got too old for playing, hang out on warm days and practice dance moves or gossip about boys (yeah, I heard that too).

Molly, I've watched you sneak cigarettes in that backyard (if you're still smoking, you should quit).

Bennie, I've watched you study for school tests in that backyard.

Take me there.

Inside this bag is a scattering tube with my ashes. Take me there, and let me stay where my proudest, greatest adventure and accomplishment ever was. That backyard, where I watched you both grow up.

There are also two necklaces in this bag with some of my ashes. One for each of you. So that no matter where you go, I'll be with you for every adventure.

I hope this trip has taught you how to love, understand, forgive, and, most importantly, how to live. I hope it has taught you to seek friendship in even the most unexpecting places. I hope it's taught you how important it is to create a legacy for yourself and be kind as much as possible. There is not one day promised to us. We have to make sure we live that way. The only thing promised about this story that we create for ourselves is that it comes to an end.

I love both of you so much.

Forever and always,

Dad.

Molly and Bennie were sobbing. Molly clutched the letter to her chest. Oddly, this was the last thing she had of her dad—the last communication she would ever receive. She reached into the bag and pulled out the scattering tube covered in the design of a map.

Through the tears, Molly and Bennie laughed. It was perfect.

She reached into the bag again and pulled out the two necklaces. They were sterling silver with heart-shaped lockets. She handed one to Bennie, who put it on, clasping it behind her neck.

When the tears settled a bit, they headed back toward home. No GPS needed.

They pulled into the driveway, and Molly smiled at the sight of her car—something familiar. This time, being in the driveway didn't feel so foreign. In fact, she felt like she was right where she was supposed to be.

They got out and walked to the white picket fence, opening the gate. As they stepped into the backyard, Molly took a good look. The nighttime summer sky was rolling in, a perfect blend of purples, oranges and pinks, just like the nights she would play with Bennie as kids.

She looked at the old oak tree that sat at the very edge of the yard, remembering it being "base" when they would play tag. She could practically taste the chicken cutlets her dad would make for dinner, practically hear the giggles of two little girls who were so innocently naïve.

She reached into the bag and pulled out the scattering tube.

"Are you ready?" she asked Bennie.

Bennie nodded silently.

Both sisters held one hand on the scattering tube. Molly took her other hand and opened the top. Walking together and fighting tears, they gently scattered the ashes throughout the backyard.

"I love you, Dad," Molly whispered, watching the ashes disperse.

***

One Year Later

Jacey and Molly sat on the front porch swing of her childhood home on a late spring afternoon, sipping a glass of wine and eating cheesecake that Ruth had shipped. Jax slept under the swing, gently purring and soaking up the sun. He wasn't usually an outdoor cat, but he never left the porch, which had become his favorite spot.

Molly couldn't afford the house alone. Jacey, tired of living with her parents and eager for new beginnings, happily agreed to be Molly's new roommate.

"God, this cheesecake is to *die* for," Jacey swooned.

"I told you!"

Molly's phone rang. "Oh, Bennie's Face Timing me!"

She answered the call, her face popping up on the screen.

"Hey!" Molly said.

"Hi! What are you up to?"

"Just sitting here with Jacey and drinking some wine." She aimed the screen so Jacey was in the picture.

"Hi!" Jacey waved.

"Hey, Jacey! I need you to meet someone formally." Bennie turned the phone. "This is Luis!"

"Nice to see your face, Luis!" Jacey laughed.

"Nice to see yours, too!"

Molly turned the phone back to her. "How are you doing out there?"

"Best decision I've ever made. Miss you tons, though."

"I miss you, too! What are you up to next weekend? Going to Patty's?" Molly grinned, knowing the answer.

"Oh God, no. I still haven't gone since that night."

"I won't let her!" Molly heard Luis say in the background jokingly.

"Well, if you two aren't doing anything, I'm off of school for spring break next week. I'd love to come visit."

Molly enrolled in school a few months after taking over the house. After her trip with Bennie, she decided she wanted to get into counseling—specifically grief counseling. She finally felt like she'd found her passion.

"Yeah! We'll be here! Come visit! Jacey can come, too!"

"I have become the designated pet sitter!" Jacey giggled.

"I'm sure I can work something out for Jax," Molly said. "I've made friends with the D'Angelos next door. They won't mind taking care of him."

"Alright, well, let me know your plan!" Bennie said. "We're about to go out to dinner. I'll talk to you soon. Love you!"

"Love you more."

Jacey put her feet down to stop the swing. "I'm going to make some dinner. You hungry?"

"Yes. I'll be in. Just give me a minute to finish up this glass."

"Alrighty."

As Jacey went inside, Molly looked out at the front yard and saw a woman pushing a stroller and walking her poodle mix.

"Hello!" Molly called out, waving.

"Hi! Beautiful today, isn't it?" the woman said, smiling and waving back.

"Absolutely! Your dog is adorable!"

"Thank you!"

Jax had come out from underneath the swing, stalking something. Molly leaned down to see what Jax was looking at when he pounced, laid on his back, and began batting playfully in the air at a white butterfly. She laughed as she watched him. He twisted and turned, batting at the butterfly gracefully as if to tell it that he was only playing.

Adventure is everywhere, as long as you're looking for it.

She couldn't wait to see what adventures this home would have for her. She couldn't wait to see her children playing in the backyard one day—making up silly games, thinking they were sneaky. She couldn't wait to cook dinner for them, watching them grow.

She couldn't wait to see how beautiful her story would be. This time, she would appreciate every small adventure in between.

A Note from The Author

Since I was a kid, I have always had a passion for writing and reading and dreamt of writing a book. I have also always had a passion for travel, adventures, and exploring.

I started writing Chasing Letters in December of 2022. I was trying to write about places that I had never seen and describe them through pictures on the internet. Unsurprisingly, I was having a difficult time.

I wanted to bring my readers with me on these adventures and decided that the only way I'd be able to do that is by seeing these places for myself. So, I went and visited each place that I wrote about. Many of the characters you met are based on people I've met through my own travels.

To My Mom, Susan, for always encouraging me to chase my wildest dreams – thank you. I owe my accomplishments and bravery to you.

To my husband and adventure partner, Zac, who has been my backbone throughout this entire process and poured nothing but love and confidence into me. Thank you for everything. I love adventuring the world with you.

To my friends and family who have rooted me on and watched me step-by-step as I go after my dream, thank you. You all are absolute rockstars.

And to the reader. I hope you enjoyed reading this book as much as I enjoyed writing it, and I'm grateful that you gave it a chance.
Thank you.

Made in the USA
Middletown, DE
20 September 2023

38653931R00236